The
Lodger

GEORGES SIMENON
The Lodger

Translated from the French
by Stuart Gilbert

A Helen and Kurt Wolff Book
Harcourt Brace Jovanovich, Publishers
San Diego   New York   London

Library of Congress Cataloging in Publication Data

Simenon, Georges, 1903–
   The lodger.

   Translation of: Le locataire.
   "A Helen and Kurt Wolff book."
   I. Title.
PQ2637.I53L613   1983   843'.912   83–212
ISBN 0–15–152960–4

Printed in the United States of America

Designed by Mark Likgalter

First American edition 1983

B C D E

The
Lodger

1

"For heaven's sake shut the window!" groaned Elie, pulling the blankets up to his chin. "Have you gone crazy?"

"But the air's so bad in here." Sylvie's form showed in white relief against the grayness of the window. "You were sweating all last night, and the place smells like a sickroom."

He snuffled, and inched down lower in the bed, curling his lean limbs into a ball, while the girl stepped into the warm glow of the bathroom and turned on the faucets. For some minutes the hiss of water made further talk out of the question. One eye emerged from the sheets, and Elie contemplated now the window, now the bathroom. The light outside was cheerless, and the sight of the open window sent a shiver down his spine each time he looked toward it. That morning early risers must have been greeted by a snowstorm, but it was now eleven and no more flakes were falling from the sallow clouds hanging low above the housetops of Brussels. The streetlights on Avenue du Jardin Botanique had been left on, and shop windows, too, were lighted up.

From where he lay, Elie had a clear view over the black, gleaming avenue, up and down which streetcars were gliding in slow, clanging files. And he could also see the Botanical

Gardens, sheeted with snow, the pond frozen over except for a small black patch of open water, in which three swans sat motionless.

"Aren't you getting up?"

"Can't you see I'm ill?"

They had stayed until three in the morning at the Merryland cabaret, though all evening Elie had been blowing his nose till the tears streamed from his eyes, and imploring her to return to the hotel. It was a nasty cold, the kind that easily develops into bronchitis or flu. He felt naked and defenseless in a hostile world, sweat oozing from every pore.

"Do please shut that window, Sylvie."

After turning off the faucets she walked across the room to the window. The bathroom mirror was coated with steam.

"I'll bet old Van der Boomp is sleeping late this morning. Isn't it funny he should be staying at the Palace, too, and in the room next to ours?"

But Elias Nagear—since coming to Belgium he had accepted, not without some secret pleasure, the abbreviation of his name to "Elie"—wasn't in a mood to find anything "funny," and he grunted in a surly way:

"Damn Van der Boomp! I'm sure it's because of him you kept me hanging around that wretched bar till three in the morning."

"Don't be ridiculous!"

He knew better, but it wasn't worth arguing about. When, toward midnight, they had entered the Merryland, the room had been practically empty, except for a few professional dancers glumly eying their empty glasses. Under these conditions even the band seemed reluctant to strike up, and Sylvie kept yawning. But a change had come over the scene when, in the small hours, a fat Dutchman rolled in, escorted by two Belgians who were evidently introducing him to the night life of the capital. Everybody seemed to wake up, and one could have sworn the lights became brighter.

2

The Dutchman was obviously out to enjoy himself. He had a hearty, boyish laugh. A quarter of an hour after his appearance, four girls were chattering at his table, champagne was flowing freely, the smoke of exotic cigarettes and Havana cigars mingled above their heads.

Standing beside Elie at the bar, Sylvie kept looking enviously at the group.

"If you're feeling rotten, go to bed. I'm staying here."

It wasn't jealousy, but he refused to budge—perhaps just to aggravate her.

"I suppose you're staying on account of Van der Boomp?" he suggested. "Van der Boomp" was the name Sylvie had invented for the portly Dutchman. It got on her nerves to see other girls swilling champagne while she was sipping a modest gin fizz at the bar.

"I don't think much of his taste, anyhow," she whispered, after a long, appraising look at the four girls. Then, abruptly changing her mind, she added: "All right. Let's go."

When they were crossing the lobby of the Palace Hotel on their way to the elevator, they saw the swing door open and Van der Boomp roll in. So the girls hadn't been able to hold him, after all! Sylvie thought better of him at once, and when, in the elevator, he shot obviously admiring glances at her, her opinion of him rose still higher.

But she had had to spend the night with Nagear, who was now gazing at her from the bed with puffy, red-rimmed eyes, his nose swollen, his cheeks greasy with perspiration—and who had hardly any money left.

"What on earth are you going out for?" he grumbled.

"That's my business," she replied as she drew on her stockings. "Look here! I'll need some cash."

"Nothing doing!"

So far, only the bathroom had been lighted, and the air in the bedroom seemed full of grayish dust. After fastening her black garters, Sylvie switched on the light and, while the scene outside the window blacked itself out, the objects in the room came into view.

On the dressing table, between two small pink-shaded lamps, were strewn silver-topped bottles, scent sprays, all the dainty paraphernalia of a woman's toilet.

He watched the whiteness of her breasts vanish beneath a gauzy silk chemise, and heard her voice again:

"You have a few hundred francs left, surely?"

"Why don't you sell that nugget of yours?" he muttered, blowing his nose.

The touch of the handkerchief on the inflamed skin was so painful that he had to take infinite precautions.

"Don't be a fool! Do you imagine I'm going to part with *that*?"

He hadn't imagined anything. He had lost all power of imagination. All he knew was that he was perspiring freely, the bed sheets were drenched, his pajamas were sticking to his legs, and the light made his eyes smart. . . .

They had met a fortnight before on board the *Théophile-Gautier*. Sylvie was returning from Cairo, where she had been one of the show girls in a cabaret. He was on his way from Istanbul to Paris, where he hoped to make a deal in carpets—a million francs' worth, held up by Customs, which he had undertaken to clear and to dispose of.

He was not the owner of these carpets; in fact, it might be a delicate task to determine the ownership and figure out the shares of all the parties concerned—assuming all went well. For there were about a dozen middlemen, at Pera, Athens, and even Paris, who had had a finger in the pie, and the negotiations had been dragging on for months. Nagear, who had business connections in Brussels, had volunteered to see the transaction through, and he had displayed such assurance of success that he had been given an advance.

Also, they had promised him 200,000 francs more once he had cleared and sold the carpets.

Sylvie had started the voyage in second class. From the first day out, four or five men were dancing attendance on her, and she stayed on deck after dinner till two or three in the morning.

And the second day she moved into a first-class cabin. Who had paid the supplement? Not Elie, in any case, since at that stage he hadn't met her. He succeeded in doing so only just before the ship reached Naples, where, she told him, she was going to get off.

He paid her passage on to Marseilles, took her with him to Paris, and then to Brussels. They had been there for three days now, and he had already discovered that the carpet venture was quite hopeless.

To make things worse, he had fallen ill, and he had barely a thousand francs left. One eye hidden by the quilt, with the other he watched Sylvie smearing red on her lips.

"Really, I don't see what you would want to do outdoors at this hour of the morning," he said querulously.

"That's my business."

"Unless you're going to make a pass at that Dutchman . . ."

"Why not?"

But he was only pretending to be jealous. On board ship it had been a different matter; there was keen competition between the men, and all the other passengers had watched their tactics with amused interest. Then, he had really felt jealous of his rivals.

But now—he knew her too well. He had seen her at her worst, in bed in the early morning, when the freckles under her eyes showed like angry blotches, and her features, in repose, betrayed their coarseness.

"Now then!" she said, drawing the tight skirt up over her hips. "Hand over that money."

He didn't move, even when she took his wallet from his coat pocket. He watched her counting out four, five, six hundred-franc notes and slipping them into her bag. Streetcars were clanging up and down the avenue, each with its one big headlight on.

"Shall I tell them to send you up some breakfast? . . . Well, why don't you answer? What's come over you?"

No, he wouldn't answer. And the sight of that bloodshot eye peering at her made her feel uneasy; there was something malevolent in its fixity, and she would have given a lot to read his thoughts.

"See you later!" she said. He made no movement, while she flung a fur coat over her shoulders. "You might at least say *'Au revoir'* to me," she added, almost pleadingly.

After turning off the light in the bathroom, she hunted around for her gloves, then glanced out the window at the dreary view.

"Have it your own way!"

He, too, had changed. On the *Théophile-Gautier* she had been impressed by his smart appearance, and he had looked much younger than his age, which was thirty-five. He had jet-black hair and a rather prominent nose.

"Are you a Turk?" she had asked at their first meeting.

"Not really. I'm of Portuguese origin."

She had found him good company; or, rather, he had a knack of making unexpected, cynical remarks, and seemed to have knocked around the world—and the half-world, too. When she told him she was a dancer, he had asked in which of the Cairo cabarets she had performed.

"At the Tabarin."

"Ah, yes. A thousand francs a month, *plus* a rake-off on the fizz."

That was so. Evidently he knew Cairo. He also knew Bucharest, where she had been, at Maxim's, for two months. He had amusing tales to tell about the men with whom she'd taken up.

"You're rich, aren't you?"

"I'll draw 200,000 francs the day I reach Brussels."

And now—all that was over. He was a sick man, on his beam-ends—and ugly into the bargain! The glamour had departed.

"*Au revoir.*"

She left her luggage in the bedroom. As she passed Van der Boomp's door she threw a quick glance at it and saw the mail slot crammed with fat Dutch newspapers.

Elie hardly noticed when she went out. He stared at the ceiling, then at the window, then at the unlighted lamps. He started to blow his nose, but the feel of the handkerchief on the raw skin made him wince. Beads of sweat were oozing from his chest and trickling along his ribs.

Sylvie was saying to the hall porter:

"Get me a car, please."

"A taxi?"

"Well, it's for the suburbs—Charleroi."

"Oh, in that case I'll call up a rental car, and you can arrange a price with the chauffeur."

All the lights were on in the lobby, and Sylvie whiled away the time inspecting the showcases of local shops lined up along the walls. Soon she stepped into a car driven by a liveried chauffeur.

"Take me to Bon Marché first."

It was so dark outside that one could hardly believe the hour was noon. In Bon Marché all the frosted-glass globes were lighted. Gusts of icy air kept pouring in through the revolving doors, and the girls behind the counters had sweaters on under their black blouses.

Sylvie seemed uncertain about what she wanted. Finally she bought a pair of blue leather slippers, a sweater, two pipes, some stockings, and a vanity bag. In her heavy fur she looked like a wealthy lady, and when a girl followed her out, carrying the parcels to the car, she explained:

"They're presents."

The snow was sticking in the woods bordering the Charleroi

7

road, and it was colder here than in the city. The windows of the car grew misted, and Sylvie wiped them with her gloved hand. When the first collieries and miners' cottages came in sight, she pressed her forehead to the glass.

As the car was entering Charleroi she opened her bag, took out a mirror, and skillfully revived her make-up.

"Turn left," she said. "Now left again. Cross the bridge. Then follow the streetcar tracks."

A rash of snow mottled the flanks of the tall black heaps beside the coal pits. The road was a long, dreary vista of mean houses, all exactly alike, their brick walls black with coal dust. Now and then a line of skips traveling on an aerial cable rattled overhead, and sometimes a miniature train crawled across the road, preceded by a man with a red flag.

It was neither town nor country. Here and there the rows of houses gave way to what might have been a field, but on a closer view proved to be a pithead. The air throbbed with the noise of engines; it was like driving through an immense factory.

"Stop at Number 53."

There was nothing to distinguish it from the other houses. In the front window, between white lace curtains, stood a copper pot in which a nondescript green plant languished. The chauffeur was about to ring when Sylvie said:

"No. Bring the packages."

Peeping through the keyhole, she rattled the mail slot. A woman in her forties opened the door and, drying her hands on her blue apron, stared at the visitor.

"Don't you recognize me, Ma?"

Sylvie kissed her. Her mother submitted to the kiss, showing no more emotion than a mild astonishment; then she gazed at the packages in the chauffeur's arms.

"What's all them things?"

"Oh, some little presents . . . Hand them over, Jacques. You can go and have your lunch now. Come back in an hour."

The kitchen door at the far end of the hall stood open, and a young man could be seen with his feet in the oven, a book propped on his knees.

"That's Monsieur Moise," the woman said as she and Sylvie entered the kitchen. Then, with what seemed a slight reluctance, she explained to the young man: "This is my daughter, who's just back from Egypt. . . . It *was* Egypt, wasn't it, where you were last?"

But Moise had already edged his way past them and was hurrying upstairs.

"So you still have lodgers?" Sylvie remarked.

"How do you think we'd make both ends meet without 'em?"

A big saucepan was simmering on the range beside the coffeepot, which was always kept full to the brim. Sylvie had dropped her coat across a chair, and her mother was surreptitiously pawing the fur.

"Why did you tell the driver to come back?"

"Because I'll have to be off again soon."

"Oh, will you?"

As she always did when somebody dropped in, Madame Baron poured out a cup of coffee. She was in her working clothes: shabby black dress, big blue apron. Sylvie unwrapped the slippers and handed them to her mother.

"Like them?"

Her mother sniffed and shook her head.

"What would I want with things like that? I'd look silly in 'em."

"Where's Antoinette?"

"Cleaning the rooms."

No sooner had she spoken than Antoinette came down the stairs carrying a pail and a mop. For a moment she stared at her sister, then exclaimed:

"Gosh!"

"What did you say?"

9

"I said 'Gosh!' You *are* dolled up! Got a job in the movies?"

They dabbed their lips to each other's cheeks. Antoinette's eyes fell on the blue slippers.

"Are they for me?"

"Well, I'd meant them for Ma, but since she doesn't want them . . . I've brought you some stockings and underwear. Look!"

Sylvie opened the other packages, but without much interest. A pipe rolled out and smashed to the floor.

"Will Pa be back soon?"

"Not till tonight. He's on the Ostend express now. You'll wait to see him, won't you?"

"Not today. But I'll be coming again."

Her mother was eying her shrewdly. Perched on a chair, her sister had pulled up her skirt, displaying her thin legs, and was trying on the stockings. There was a smell of soup, a sound of water boiling, the comfortable drone of a well-fed fire.

"All your rooms rented?"

"Didn't you see the card in the window? The ground-floor room's empty—the most expensive one, needless to say. Nowadays foreigners don't seem to have no money. You saw Monsieur Moise just now; well, he has to come and study in the kitchen because he can't afford a fire in his room. Set the table, Antoinette. We'll have a snack before the lodgers come."

"So you still give them board?"

"There's two come every day for lunch. If I didn't feed 'em, they'd be always plaguing me for hot water to make coffee and boil eggs, and messing up their rooms with pots and pans."

Madame Baron was a stout, short-legged woman. Antoinette, who was shorter and thinner than her elder sister, had a quaint, birdlike little face, pale-blue laughing eyes.

"So you've taken to using rouge?" her elder sister observed.

"Why shouldn't I? *You* make up all right."

"It doesn't suit you. At your age . . ."

10

"When you were my age you did lots of other things!"

Her mother was straining the soup on a corner of the range. Beyond the window was a small back yard, and big drops of melted snow were dripping from the eaves.

Shielding his mouth with his hand, the porter at the Palace murmured into the telephone:

"Is that you, Monsieur Van der Cruyssen? There's a gentleman here, a Monsieur Blanqui, who would like to see you. Shall I send him up? . . . Would you go up, sir? Room 413, fourth floor."

Elie had managed to drag himself out of the sodden bed. His throat swathed in a scarf, slippers on his feet, he was prowling around the room, at loose ends. He had heard someone talking on the phone in the next room. For some moments he stood at the window idly gazing at the snowbound city, the pond in the Botanical Gardens, the three half-frozen swans. The din of streetcars and car horns jarred in his aching head.

"Come in."

The voice was in the next room. On occasion the two bedrooms formed part of a suite, and there was only a locked door between them. The voices in the adjoining room could be heard as distinctly as the clanging of the streetcars.

"Good morning, Monsieur Van der Cruyssen. Sorry to be so late, but I had to stop at the bank. . . ."

Elie listened with half an ear. He felt hot and cold all over. It struck him that a hot bath might do him good, but he hadn't the energy to go about it.

"So you've decided to leave tonight?" the voice went on.

"Yes. I'm taking the last train to Paris. . . . What will you have to drink? A glass of port?"

A voice could be heard giving an order on the telephone to the wine waiter.

When that was done, Elie followed suit: he, however,

ordered a hot toddy. Catching sight of his face in the mirror, he was appalled by its ugliness. But that might be because he hadn't shaved, and the mauve scarf emphasized the sallowness of his skin, the dark half-moons under his eyes.

"As you wished, I've taken the money in French notes."

Elie bent down and put an eye to the keyhole. He saw a small man, who looked like an accountant or a broker, laying on the table ten bundles of notes.

"Count them, please."

Van der Cruyssen (Elie still thought of him as "Van der Boomp") was in a black dressing gown and scarlet slippers. He counted the notes, flicking them expertly, like one who is used to handling large sums of paper money. Then he placed them in a pigskin attaché case.

"Come in."

A waiter entered, carrying a bottle of port, another of rum, and a glass of hot water. These last were for Elie, who stepped back from the communicating door and, in his turn, called: "Come in."

The midday meal was beginning at the Barons'. Madame Baron stayed on her feet, waiting on her daughters and the lodgers, Domb and Valesco, who had just come back. The two young men eyed Sylvie with frank admiration. She seemed amused by the impression she was making and her sister's furious glances in her direction.

"Do you know Bucharest?" asked Plutarc Valesco, who was a Rumanian.

"I should think I do! What's more, I know nearly all your cabinet ministers."

"A delightful place, isn't it?"

"Not too bad—only everybody's stone-broke . . ."

Sitting on the arm of an easy chair, Elie sipped his hot toddy and gazed down at the avenue, swarming now with the lunch-hour crowd. Tiny snowflakes were beginning to float down from the sullen yellow sky.

"*Au revoir* then. Hope you'll have a good time in Paris."

"Thanks. See you next Wednesday."

There followed a sound of running water in Van der Boomp's bathroom. . . .

Nightfall came early, at half past three, and found Elie lying on the bed, staring at the ceiling, which was dappled with roving gleams thrown up from the street below.

At four the hall porter saw him going out, and noticed that he hadn't shaved. In fact, he had an unusually bedraggled appearance, perhaps because he hadn't troubled to get out a clean shirt.

"If Madame comes back while you're out, sir, is there any message?"

"No, thanks. I'll be back soon."

His cheeks were flushed; he looked like a man in the last stages of consumption.

The headlights showed a drab expanse of muddy road and the low branches of dripping trees. The glass behind the chauffeur's seat was open, and he said to Sylvie over his shoulder:

"I have a brother living at Marcinelle, near Charleroi. I thought you wouldn't be in a hurry, so I looked him up."

"What's his job?"

"Oh, nothing much. He's employed at the gasworks."

As they neared Brussels there were lighted cafés fringing the road, and the car skirted stands on which loomed the dark, white-helmeted forms of traffic policemen.

"Monsieur Nagear has just gone out," the porter told Sylvie as she walked toward the elevator.

"Oh? Did he leave any message?"

At eight he was still out, and she went down to the grill room to eat. Van der Boomp was at a table nearby, and she noticed that he kept trying to catch her eye as she ate the lobster salad of which her repast consisted. But, to her surprise, when she went out and started strolling around the lobby, lingering in front of the showcases, he did not come up and speak to her.

She went up to the bedroom, and after a while there was a sound of suitcases being closed in the next room, and she heard Van der Boomp say:

"No, the places in the sleeping cars are all taken. A first-class *couchette*, please. Get me one facing the engine if you can."

She changed her dress lackadaisically; she was feeling tired and, perhaps, a little depressed. There was still no sign of Elie. She counted the money remaining in her bag: 115 francs.

Still undecided what to do, she walked to the elevator. Near the street door she paused to hand the room key to the porter.

"A shame, isn't it, that he's leaving," the man remarked familiarly.

"Why?"

"He asked me who you were. Mighty taken with you, he is, that Dutchman. But he can't stand the sight of Monsieur Nagear."

She shrugged her shoulders and leaned forward for him to light her cigarette. Van der Boomp emerged from the elevator, hesitated for a moment, then came up to the porter, saying to Sylvie:

"Excuse me."

"So you're leaving us tonight, sir?"

"I have to." He emphasized the words, looking straight at Sylvie; then he handed the man some crumpled notes he had been holding ready for him. "But I'll be back next week."

He took a few steps forward, hesitated again, and finally, with a vague wave of his hand, stepped out onto the sidewalk.

"He's a businessman from Amsterdam," the porter informed Sylvie. "Rolling in it, I'd say. He comes here every Wednesday. So if you're still here next week . . ."

Her eyelashes fluttered. But all she said was:

"When Monsieur Nagear comes back, say I'm at the Merry-land. . . . No, don't tell him anything. That'll teach him a lesson! Page! Get me a taxi, please."

The snow was coming down steadily now, in big flakes that melted as soon as they touched the sidewalk. Trains were whistling, a hundred yards away, in Gare du Nord.

2

It was while he was standing on the sidewalk on Rue Neuve, jostled by the crowd and gazing into a tobacconist's window, with a shrill-voiced urchin hawking lottery tickets at his elbow, that suddenly it dawned on Elie how very far he had traveled since leaving his home in Istanbul. The tobacconist's window was packed with boxes of cigars and cigarettes of every brand, and among the latter he saw some white boxes bearing the name "Abdullah."

At Pera the most fashionable restaurant on the main thoroughfare is also called Abdullah. On the eve of his departure Elie had eaten there with friends. He knew almost everyone, shook hands at every table.

"I'm off to France tomorrow."

"Lucky devil!"

And now, standing at the corner on Rue Neuve, his hands in his coat pockets, try as he might, somehow he couldn't recall the Abdullah restaurant. Not that he had any trouble in remembering its appearance. But that was not what he was after. He wanted to recapture the atmosphere and, still more, his mood that evening.

Why, for instance, had he set out on this long journey even

though he had guessed from the start that the carpets deal was bound to fail? And why had he pretended to be so cocksure, telling everybody he knew, with a triumphant air:

"I'm on to a good thing, and I'm sailing for Marseilles tomorrow"?

All along the main street of Pera, where people were strolling in the cool of the evening, he had buttonholed acquaintances and imparted the great news.

Now, all that seemed so remote, so unreal, that he could imagine it a dream. Reality was the here and now: slushy sidewalks, a biting wind, fever, a sore nose, a dull ache between his shoulder blades.

He entered the tobacconist's.

"A pack of Turkish cigarettes, please."

The small blue jet of a gas cigar lighter danced before his eyes. The tobacconist was pink and plump. Dark forms scudded past outside the window. A pack was handed to him.

"Those aren't Turkish."

"They're Egyptian. Much better."

"There's no tobacco in Egypt."

"No tobacco in Egypt! That's a good one!"

"It's a fact," he said to the fat Belgian, who was glaring at him indignantly. "What you call Egyptian tobacco is all imported from Turkey and Bulgaria."

Wondering what had possessed him to tell the man all this, he stepped out of the shop, plunged again into the crowd, and walked, or, rather, splashed his way, ahead. Now and again he stopped in front of a shop window, usually one with a mirror, in which he could take stock of his appearance.

He was wearing a camel's-hair overcoat, an elegant felt hat, a well-cut suit.

Why did it suddenly strike him that he was a pitiable sight? Was it because of a two-day growth of beard, or his red, swollen nose and puffy cheeks? In any case, he was shocked by the face confronting him—"like death warmed up," he muttered with a wry smile. When someone brushed against him, he winced and gave a stifled cry, as if he had been dealt a blow.

He was looking for a jeweler's, but passed three before finally going into one. There he placed on the counter a lump of gold shaped like a walnut—Sylvie's "nugget." She had carried it around with her everywhere on her travels during the last two years, as a stand-by in case she was stranded in some foreign town.

The jeweler gave him 1,300 Belgian francs for it, and Elie found himself back in the street with many empty hours before him.

He could recall nothing of the voyage to Marseilles; or, rather, he remembered it as if it had been an experience in a previous life, or something in a book. Nothing had reality for him but this bleak darkness of unfriendly streets, this alien city of Brussels, with its narrow sidewalks, off which he had to step every other moment to avoid bumping into someone, these shop windows so chock-full of food that it made his gorge rise to see them, cafés with livid marble-topped tables that looked like fallen tombstones. . . .

He wasn't thinking: I'll do this; then I'll do that. Yet he had a feeling he was about to do something, and he had a notion what that something was. He was in a quarrelsome mood; he'd shown it already over the "Egyptian" cigarettes. Now he showed it again over a hot toddy.

He had entered a café on Place de Brouckère. The room reminded him of the big waiting room of a railway station. In the center stood an enormous tankard of beer, twenty feet high, brimming over with white froth, and around it some two or three hundred people were seated at small tables. A band was playing; there was a constant clatter of mugs and saucers. Waiters were dashing back and forth.

Elie ordered a hot toddy.

"Our toddies are made with wine, sir."

"I want one with rum."

"It's against the law to sell spirits in quantities of less than a quart."

"All right. Give me a quart of rum."

"This is a café, not a wine store."

"Oh, go to the devil!"

To make things worse, the lights in the room were so bright that they made his eyes smart, and there was no shelter from the glare. After some moments he walked out. Back on the street his fingers made the movement of clenching something in his pocket. On Boulevard Adolphe-Max he stopped in front of a hardware shop, the windows of which were full of tools as highly polished as the silverware in a jeweler's window. Going up to the clerk, he said without the least hesitation:

"I want a wrench."

He chose a very large one, and swung it to gauge its weight as if it were a hammer, not a wrench. It was an American make, and it cost him sixty-two francs.

He was sweating freely under his coat. And at the same time he was shivering with cold. It was the same with hunger; he felt ravenous, but every time he started to enter a restaurant or a pastry shop he felt nauseated.

"All the winning numbers of the national lottery! All the winners!"

The crowds in the street gave him the impression of a demented herd, stampeding in all directions. He gazed at the portraits of stars in the lobbies of movie houses and remembered having met one of them in Istanbul; he was one of a group of young men who had shown her around the town one evening. But that, too, seemed like an incident in a half-forgotten dream.

He knew what time the train left, but went to the station just to make sure. Yes; 12:33.

At midnight the station was empty, dimly lighted and full of grayish dust, because sweepers were at work.

"Paris. First class."

"Return, sir?"

He hesitated. He hadn't thought of that.

"Yes, a return, please."

He stopped beside the cart of the woman renting pillows, and took two of them, and a blanket. There were only ten people on the platform waiting for the train. The station was strangely quiet. Far down the line an engine was shunting, in a maze of red and yellow lights. Sudden gusts of cold wind swept the platform.

Elie noticed a porter from the Palace holding a place in one of the *couchette* sleepers, entered the same compartment, placed his pillows and blanket on the opposite seat, and sat down.

He was quite calm.

As he stepped into the compartment Van der Boomp gave Elie a quick glance, and presumably recognized him as the young man he had seen at the cabaret. But he took no more notice of him.

There were four berths, two lower and two upper, but since they were the only passengers in the compartment, the upper ones were not let down. It was pure chance that there were so few passengers—but Elie felt no surprise. It was as if he had known everything beforehand.

Van der Boomp began by putting the attaché case under his pillow. Then he opened a suitcase, took from it a navy-blue smoking jacket, a pair of travel slippers, and a bottle of mineral water.

He was a heavily built man, with a blotchy complexion and fair hair, thinning over the temples.

"Tickets, please."

The train was starting. When Van der Boomp held out his ticket, the conductor remarked:

"Were the sleeping cars full, sir?"

He evidently knew the Dutchman, and addressed him with

respectful familiarity. He hardly glanced at Elie as he punched his ticket.

"Good night, gentlemen."

Before leaving the compartment he drew down the blinds.

In his smoking jacket and slippers Van der Boomp went off to the lavatory, taking his attaché case with him, under his arm. On his return he stretched himself on the berth, took a mouthful of the mineral water, and gargled before swallowing it; then he placed the bottle on the floor beside him, within easy reach.

After a final glance at Elie, who was lying, fully dressed, on the opposite berth, he had moved the switch over to night light. The train was gathering speed, and though the compartment was overheated, icy drafts were forcing their way through invisible chinks.

Elie's right hand was clenched on the big wrench, but actually his mind was empty of thoughts. Through half-closed eyes he could see the bulb of the blue night light overhead, bathing the compartment in a dim, spectral light.

The noises of the train settled into a steady rhythm, with a ground bass of low-pitched rumblings, like the pedal notes of an organ.

Van der Boomp's mouth was open and he was breathing heavily, with an occasional snore. One of his hands dangled over the side of the berth: a chubby pink hand on whose fingers glinted a gold wedding ring and a signet ring of platinum.

Elie's gaze settled on the wedding ring, but it conveyed nothing to his mind. A sudden draft made him turn up the collar of his camel's-hair coat, and he began to perspire heavily.

The train slowed down. There was a sound of voices, hurried footsteps, and yellow light came in spurts through the chinks at the edges of the blinds, while a voice could be heard above the din, shouting out the name of the station:

"Mons!"

A panting woman scrambled into another compartment in the same car and could be heard slamming her baggage onto the rack.

Elie awoke when someone flung the door open and called: "Frontier! All passports ready, please!"

Propped on an elbow, Van der Boomp held his out.

"Thank you, sir."

Elie showed his, and the man flicked the pages over with a careless finger.

"Thank you."

The train started, and stopped again.

"Feignies Junction. All change for . . ."

Another man entered the compartment, and switched on the white light.

"French Customs. Have you anything to declare?"

Van der Boomp was less flushed, now that the door had been opened several times and the heat in the compartment reduced. But he still looked half-dazed, though he was awake enough to hold out a cigar case containing six fat cigars.

"All right. Nothing else? What's in that suitcase?"

"Clothes—none of them new."

Elie, who had no luggage, held out his box of cigarettes. The Customs officer went out and shut the door.

There was a hubbub of voices, shouts, footsteps, on the platform. An agitated woman could be heard inquiring shrilly of a porter:

"Is the train leaving right now?"

"No, not till thirty-two past . . ."

Elie lay down again, after switching off the white light. Van der Boomp seemed to have trouble getting off to sleep and changed his position several times. But after a quarter of an hour or so he started snoring again.

Elie's eyes were open. His hands were so wet that he could hardly grip the wrench, which was coated with a film of sweat.

He kept his eyes fixed on the small bulb overhead, the filaments of which showed white through the blue glass.

When the train rounded certain bends, his body pressed against the wall, while that of the Dutchman seemed on the point of rolling to the floor.

He turned down his coat collar, but the draft on his neck compelled him to put it up again.

"Saint-Quentin! Next stop Compiègne!"

He slipped out of the compartment into the corridor and encountered a blast of icy wind, since one of the windows was open. On the dark horizon glimmered the streetlights of a sleeping town.

"It hasn't snowed here," Elie murmured.

He paced the corridor from end to end. The blinds were down in all the compartments. He visited the lavatory, but the tension of his nerves was such that he could do no more than look at his reflection in the glass.

When he got back to the compartment, the train was moving again. Van der Boomp was still snoring, the leather attaché case beneath his head creaking faintly under its weight.

Elie lit a cigarette. The match flame did not evoke the slightest tremor on the sleeper's face.

It was impossible to say at what moment he finally nerved himself to do it. He took some puffs on his cigarette, and the smoke had a peculiar flavor that he recognized at once—the taste it always had when he was suffering from a cold. He shot a quick glance at the blinds screening them from the corridor.

The wrench had warmed up to the temperature of his hand. The express was traveling full speed across a stretch of open country. Without rising altogether from the seat, he wriggled forward to its extreme edge. For a moment he held the wrench poised in the air, taking aim at the center of the man's skull. Then he brought it down with all his might.

What happened was so grotesque that he felt like breaking into hysterical laughter. Very slowly the Dutchman's eyelids parted. The pupils came into view. And the look that wavered up through the dim blue light was one of blank surprise, the look of a man who can't imagine why he has been roused from sleep. And yet a trickle of blood was creeping forward through his hair, spreading across his forehead.

He tried to raise his head, to see what was happening. Elie struck again, twice, three times, ten times, infuriated by those mild, insensate eyes staring up at him.

He stopped only when his arm grew tired and he hadn't the strength to raise it again. The wrench dropped from his moist fingers, clanged on the floor. He leaned back on the cushions, gazing dully in front of him, and took a deep breath. And, while he did so, he listened intently. Was there the sound of another's breathing, besides his own, in the compartment? Fervently he hoped not! His wrist was still aching, he had no desire to start again. . . .

Without looking at the body, he went to the window and let it down, after releasing the blind. There had been no snow at Saint-Quentin, but here, he noticed, the fields were white as far as eye could see, and the sky had a frosty sheen.

His coat kept getting in his way and he flung it off. Then, trying not to look at the Dutchman's head, he raised the body, intending to heave it out the window onto the tracks. He made three attempts. Contrary to all his preconceived ideas, the body was limp, and folded up when he tried to move it.

When Elie finally let go, the upper part of the body was trailing on the floor, while the legs remained on the berth.

And then panic haste came over him. He put on his overcoat, opened the attaché case, and thrust the bundles of notes into his pockets. He couldn't bear to stay a moment longer in the compartment. Without even stopping to close the window, he hurried out into the corridor. As he walked through the concertina vestibule leading to the next car, a rush of icy air enveloped him and he saw blobs of ice on the iron stanchions.

From car to car he made his way the full length of the train, not stopping until he reached the door of the baggage car.

Only then the thought occurred to him: "I forgot to shut the window. Someone will see him when we get to Compiègne."

The blinds were drawn everywhere, and he didn't dare enter any of the compartments. Finally he shut himself up in a lavatory, where the light was so bright that it made his eyes smart. He looked around for a switch to turn it off, but couldn't find one. There was a mirror over the basin and, try as he might, he could not help gazing at his face.

"I forgot to shut the window. . . . I forgot to shut the window. . . . I forgot . . ." The words kept echoing in his head, timing themselves to the thudding of the wheels.

"And when we get to Compiègne . . . When we get to Compiègne . . ."

He put down the lid and sat on it, crossing his legs and leaning back against the wall.

When the train stopped, he jumped up with a start, for he had fallen asleep. He heard shouts on the platform. But he was too worn out to move. Every limb was aching and he could feel the fever of his blood. After a few moments the train started again.

"When we get to Compiègne . . ." No, that was silly. They had just left Compiègne. In an hour they would be at Paris.

He had no plans. He didn't even try to concoct one. All he wanted was to lie down and sleep. But that absurd jingle was running in his fuddled brain: "I forgot to shut the window. . . . And when we get to Compiègne . . ."

By now they must be quite near Paris, crossing the outer suburbs. With a great effort he struggled to his feet, went out of the lavatory, and pressed his face to a window. Blocks of tall, five-story apartment houses loomed up beside the line, against a background of vague fields. There were some lighted windows, probably those of rooms where workers lived who had to make an early start.

No one was in the corridor. Then a railway employee appeared at the far end and walked past without looking at him. The glass was so cold that he took his forehead from it; it seemed to be freezing his brain.

"I forgot to shut the window . . . to shut the window . . ."

Someone dived into the lavatory and the door hit Elie in the back. There was a sound of running water. A woman came up and tried to open the door, in spite of the notice: "Engaged."

Then came a series of tunnels. Elie had a brief glimpse of a brightly lighted streetcar swinging up a muddy street. Here, too, there was no snow.

A countrywoman, laden with bundles, stepped out into the corridor and took her stand beside him. The train was slowing down; it was entering Gare du Nord, and its rumble swelled to a hollow roar under the high vaulted roof.

Before it stopped, Elie opened the door and stopped on the step. The woman behind him tapped him on the shoulder.

"Be careful."

He jumped off, but he was not the first to alight. Already a passenger was hurrying to the Way Out, suitcase in hand. The ticket collector took his ticket without a word. Looking around, Elie saw another train, which people were boarding, on the next platform. On a sign fastened to the side of a third-class car he read: "Namur, Liège, Cologne, Berlin."

No one was watching him.

He took no thought, but started running. The train was beginning to pull out. He opened a door, swung himself in, and sank to the seat of a third-class compartment in which there were two women drinking coffee from a Thermos.

All one side of the compartment was empty, and he stretched himself full-length on the seat, wrapping his camel's-hair coat around him. When he awoke, day had dawned. A conductor was tugging at his shoulder.

"Ticket, please."

The two women, who were in black, looked at him, smiling. His ticket? For some moments he was at a loss. Then he remembered the man at the Brussels ticket office who had asked: "Return, sir?"

He felt in his pockets. His fingers groped among the wads of notes. Under them he found a small square of cardboard.

The conductor looked at the ticket, then at the passenger. "This is a first-class ticket," he said.

Obviously. Elie gave him a smile that seemed to say, "How silly of me!" And the two women understood now why he was wearing such an expensive-looking coat.

"The third car, toward the engine," the man said. "If you stay here, you'll have to get out for Customs inspection. First-class passengers are inspected in the train."

His lips were parched, and he had developed a stiff neck. The draft, most likely. He stumbled up the swaying corridor, and, pausing for a moment, saw snowbound fields dotted here and there with cottages and farmhouses, smoke rising from the chimneys.

As he crossed the metal plates between the cars he was greeted by blasts of bitterly cold air. There was an empty first, and the car had a lugubrious, almost sinister appearance in the bleak, gray light.

What could the time be? Were they near the frontier? The words started running in his head again: "When we get to Compiègne . . . When we get to Compiègne . . . ."

At all costs he must have a drink. He hurried to a lavatory. The basin was black with soot. He turned the small faucet to the right, and there was a gush of boiling water. He turned it to the left, and there came a trickle of tepid, muddy water, which he cupped in his hand and brought to his lips. It left a taste of grime and fever in his mouth.

The train stopped, and Elie hurried out, afraid of being discovered in the lavatory, and bumped into a man in a gray coat.

"Were you in this car?"

"Well . . . yes."

"Your passport, please. Thank you. Anything to declare? Any jewelry, valuables, new clothes?"

Elie shook his head.

He was half asleep. His clothes were soiled and crumpled. His handkerchief was a sodden, grimy ball.

Jeumont. Erquelinnes. Red-brick houses. Windows with snow-white curtains, ferns in copper pots. Taverns. Café de la Gare. Bistro. Khaki uniforms instead of blue.

And always, parallel with the line, the Meuse, with long strings of barges towed by stocky little tugs, whistling impatiently at the lock gates.

The door of the compartment opened. A young man in dark uniform inquired:

"Breakfast, sir? Breakfast will be served immediately after Namur."

On the point of saying, "No," Elie took the small red ticket that was handed him, reserving a seat in the dining car.

He got out at Namur. At last he knew the time. The big station clock, with a garishly white dial and hands so black that they seemed painted in India ink, informed him it was eleven.

"When's the next train to Brussels?"

"Twelve-ten."

He was too exhausted to leave the station, and settled down in the third-class waiting room, where there were the most people. Everyone had a dripping umbrella, and the floor was covered with puddles; even the varnished wooden benches had a coat of moisture.

On the far side of a glazed door white-aproned waiters were hurrying back and forth, and tables were laid. But Elie didn't feel like sitting down to a meal. He went up to the buffet and pointed to a pile of sandwiches.

"A *pistolet*?" asked the plump young woman behind the counter.

"A *'pistolet'*?" he asked irritably. "What the devil do you mean?"

"That's what we call 'em here, in Belgium."

"Why can't you call them 'sandwiches,' like everybody else? . . . All right, I'll take three."

But he managed to get through only half a sandwich as he paced up and down the third-class waiting room.

It was dark by the time the train reached Brussels, and at first he didn't recognize the station, because the train had come in at an unfamiliar platform. Outside, snow was falling, or, rather, the air was thick with melting flakes. Hotel porters were waiting at the Exit.

"Astoria." "Palace." "Grand Hotel.". . . "A taxi, sir?"

He made a detour so as not to pass the man from the Palace. Avoiding the main streets, he turned to the left, then to the left again, and found himself in a tangle of mean streets, lined with cafés and fried-fish shops.

At last he entered a café where people were sitting with cups of coffee and mugs of beer in front of them, waiting for trains apparently, since most of them had luggage.

"Do you have a telephone?"

"Yes, over there on the right. You can get a counter at the cash desk."

But what was he to do with the counter that was handed him? In Turkish cafés, counters aren't used. . . . Yet when he thought of Turkey it seemed no more than a name—the name of a country in which he'd never set foot. He held the disk up inquiringly.

"I see. You're a foreigner. What number do you want?"

"The Palace Hotel, please."

Elie picked up the receiver.

"Is this the Palace? I want to talk to Mademoiselle Sylvie. What? She's out? . . . I'll call up again soon. No; no message."

He was longing for a hot toddy, and his desire for one had

grown to an obsession. But there was nothing to be done; he resigned himself to drinking a glass of beer in a corner of the café near the telephone booth. There was a clock almost in front of him, above the bar of polished oak. When half an hour had passed he called up again; then again after another half hour.

At eight, when he called up for the sixth time, a voice said to him:

"I think I saw Mademoiselle Sylvie in the grillroom. Hold the line, please."

He pictured the Palace grillroom, with its pink-shaded lamps on the tables, flowers in cut-glass vases, the side table glistening with silver, and the big cart on which the headwaiter now was trundling from table to table the day's roast.

"Hello? Who's there?"

With his mind's eye he could see the telephone booth beside the reading room, with its big notice on the glass door: "No Smoking."

"Hello?" she called again impatiently.

He felt sure that she was wearing her green silk dress, which was so tight around the hips that he had to help her into it.

"Hello?"

He had to say something. . . .

"It's I," he whispered into the receiver.

"What! You're back, Elie? And high time, too! Why haven't you come to the hotel?"

"Ssh! Can't tell you now; I'll explain. I want you to come and meet me here. I'm at a café near the station. . . . Just a moment."

He ran out of the booth and buttonholed a waiter.

"What's the name of this place?"

"Au Bon Départ."

Back at the phone he said:

"Au Bon Départ. That's the name. You'll find it easily. But finish your dinner first."

She gave a little grunt, then murmured sulkily:

"All right, I'll come."

And by now she must be crossing the lobby, wondering what on earth he had to tell.

"Can I have something to eat?" he asked a man who seemed to be the owner of the café.

"There's only ham and pudding."

He was too hungry to bother about what the food was like. After drinking off his beer at a gulp, he wolfed what was set in front of him. If now and then he made a wry face, it was only because of twinges in his stiff neck.

Not once all day had he given a thought to the late Van der Boomp.

3

Sylvie drew back hastily. She had just paid the taxi driver, after an upward glance to make sure the name above the café entrance was the right one: Au Bon Départ. As she was stepping across a puddle on the sidewalk a dark form moved out of a patch of shadow beside the lighted doorway, and a voice whispered: "Sylvie!"

The tan overcoat and the voice reassured her. It was Elie. But, even before she saw his face, she had a feeling that in some way he was changed.

Indeed, so impressed was she that she followed him in the rain, without a word of protest, and down a narrow side street into a dismal and deserted part of the town where she had never been before.

Under the first streetlight she shot a keen glance at him, and noticed that he turned his head away.

"You do look a sight!" she exclaimed. "Why haven't you shaved?"

They moved out of the little pool of light and had another fifty yards to walk before coming to the next one. The lights were spaced out at that distance all the way down the street; the only additional light came from a small candy shop some way ahead.

Sylvie wrapped her fur coat more tightly around her. Her high heels made walking difficult, and she could feel drops of muddy water splashing her stockings and oozing through them.

"Do we have far to go?"

He looked back over his shoulder. There was no one around. A piano was tinkling in an upper room, a pink glow seeping through the curtains.

"Let's go a bit farther," he said.

He could hardly drag himself along. At one moment he linked his arm with Sylvie's, but it was no help. Perhaps they weren't walking in step, or Sylvie, hugging her fur coat to her, had her arm at the wrong angle.

She kept watching him from the corner of an eye. She had guessed that it was something serious. . . .

"Where have you been?" She realized he couldn't bring himself to speak first.

"To Paris."

He could not have explained why the rain seemed to make talking difficult, but so it was. Then he saw a dark porch some ten yards from a streetlight and drew her under its shelter. But he didn't kiss her, or take her in his arms. And anyway, her fur coat was beaded with big drops of rain.

After inspecting the street in both directions he drew a handful of notes from his pocket and showed them to the girl in gloomy silence.

She didn't realize at once, and fingered the notes incredulously.

"How much?" she asked after a brief silence.

"A hundred thousand."

She was staring not at his face but at his overcoat.

"In the train . . . ?"

They could hardly see each other. The drizzle made a haze, like a teeming cloud of gnats, around the streetlight.

"Yes. Van der Boomp."

She raised her eyes slowly, taken aback, but not overmuch, and there was an unspoken question in her gaze.

"Yes," he repeated, while in his pocket his fingers made the movement of gripping a wrench.

The wet street stretched out to infinity, gray and gleaming in the patches of lamplight.

"How about moving on?" Sylvie suggested.

Their footsteps echoed in the emptiness between the rows of houses, all exactly alike.

"It's in the newspapers, I expect," he said.

"You haven't looked at them?" She sounded surprised.

He shook his head, and she guessed he hadn't dared to buy one. There was no need for him to speak. She knew that he expected her to help him; that was why he had returned to Brussels. And she knew that he was waiting. . . .

"They're sure to be watching the borders," she murmured, as if to herself. Then added more loudly: "It's no use hanging around here. See those lights over there? There's bound to be a café of sorts."

His arms dangling at his sides, he followed her down the street. She seemed to be thinking hard. Before reaching the place where the lights were, she stopped for a moment.

"Fifty-fifty."

He understood at once and handed her the contents of one pocket, about half the money he had stolen. She put the notes in her bag.

"Oh, they're French notes," she remarked casually.

They came to a sleepy-looking café; the two billiard tables, at which nobody was playing, made the room seem emptier still. The proprietor was seated by the window, chatting with a fat, red-cheeked man; his wife was knitting at the cash desk.

"This'll do."

So homely was the atmosphere in the café, that it was like breaking in on a family party. When they walked across the room and settled down behind a billiard table, the proprietor heaved an audible sigh and rose lethargically from his chair.

"What can I get you?"

Sylvie ordered two coffees.

From then on it was she who took command; both of them seemed to accept this as a matter of course. Elie was staring at the floor, on which sawdust lay in ripples like sand on a beach. When Sylvie rose to her feet, he looked up, but didn't ask what she was going to do. She went to a rack on which were some newspapers rolled around strips of wood.

The man served them in silence. The coffee fell drop by drop from the nickel-plated filter resting on each cup. The apoplectic-looking customer blew his nose noisily.

There was a rustle of paper as Sylvie turned a page of the newspaper she was reading. She looked up to say:

"Put two lumps of sugar in my cup, please."

He did so; then drank his coffee to keep himself in countenance.

"Now—pay," she said.

The proprietor was eying them from his seat by the window, obviously wondering why these two young people had dropped in at such an hour. Sylvie rose, and Elie followed her out. After stopping on the sidewalk to get her bearings, she started off toward the central area.

"Well?"

"The conductor gave your description, but he doesn't seem to have noticed much, except that you were wearing a tan overcoat."

And promptly, Elie felt as if his overcoat were made of lead, and looked anxiously around to make sure no one was watching him.

"Another thing he said was that you had a foreign accent— but he didn't say what sort of accent."

As they walked on, Elie transferred the notes, his handkerchief, and a penknife from his overcoat pockets to those of his coat. Beside a fence running alongside a field used as a dump he paused and turned to Sylvie.

"Here?"

"No. If it's found, they'll know you're in Brussels. You'd better drop it in the canal."

"Where's that?"

"Oh, quite a ways from here."

From time to time a streetcar sped by, packed with seated, stolid figures, like museum pieces in a showcase.

"We'd better take a taxi," Sylvie said.

"Think it's safe?"

"Yes . . . I know the trick."

She hailed the first taxi that passed and said to the driver, with an affected smirk:

"Take us to the Cambre woods. Drive slowly, please."

That way he'd take them for a loving couple. There was no light in the taxi, which creaked at every joint. Elie slipped out of his overcoat—after which neither of them made the least movement.

"Is there water?" he asked under his breath.

"Yes, a big pond. You'll have to put stones in the pockets to make sure of its sinking."

The woods were completely empty. From the leafless branches overhead big drops flashed down in front of the headlights. After they had gone a mile or so, Sylvie tapped on the sliding window between them and the driver, and the taxi stopped.

"We're going for a stroll. We'll be back in five minutes."

The driver hesitated, swung his shoulders around and bent toward her, whispering something Elie failed to catch. As they walked away, he asked what the man had said.

"Oh, he suggested we should stay in the taxi while *he* went for a walk."

But neither smiled. They groped about for stones. For appearance' sake, Sylvie had linked her arm in Elie's. She prodded a big stone with the toe of her shoe.

"Pick it up."

It was chilly in the woods, and in his gray suit Elie felt the cold. His teeth were chattering. The darkness was heavy with the fumes of damp earth and leaves.

"That one, too . . . Put your arm around me. He may be watching."

They climbed over the low railings around the pond. The ground fell away toward the water. Sylvie held Elie's hand while he bent forward as far as he could. There was only a faint splash, but they looked around nervously. The driver might have followed them, suspecting suicide.

They started back, Elie in front. Sylvie plucked at his sleeve.

"Not so fast. We don't look like a loving couple."

In the taxi she said, as if it had just struck her:

"Feeling cold?"

"A little. But it doesn't matter."

His lips were blue. Now and again his shoulders shook convulsively, and, to make things worse, he was continually rubbing against Sylvie's damp fur coat.

"Now I'll tell you what to do," she said in a low tone. "You must take the train to Charleroi. . . ."

He shook his head emphatically.

"I won't take a train."

"Well, a car if you prefer. When you get to Charleroi go to Number 53, Rue du Laveu; it's a house where they rent furnished rooms. I happen to know that there's one vacant." He looked at her wonderingly, but asked no question.

"My people live there," Sylvie explained. "You can tell Mother that it's I who sent you. You'd better say you've got into trouble in your country—over politics, or something like that—and want to lie low for a bit. Pay three months in advance. That way Mother'll keep her mouth shut if the police come snooping around."

They were back in Brussels, and the driver kept looking around, waiting to be told where to go.

"To the Merryland," Sylvie said.

"But—but I can't go in like this."

"Of course not. You mustn't come with me. But I've got to go there. I have a date."

He made no protest. Docile as a child, he let her decide for him. However, he ventured to ask:

"Will you be staying in Brussels?"

"Yes, but I'll come to see you." She puckered her brows, thinking hard. "Listen! Perhaps you'd better not tell Mother I sent you. Pretend not to know me. Once you've given her the money, you won't have any trouble."

"But how shall I get news of you?"

"I'll write now and then to Antoinette. She's my sister. She'll talk about my letters at meals, and since you'll all eat at the same table . . ."

The taxi had stopped. The Merryland doorman opened the door and held a big umbrella over Sylvie as she stepped out. Sitting well back in the far corner, Elie was almost invisible.

"Au revoir," said Sylvie.

She didn't kiss him. Bending forward, but with her head outside the door, she groped with her hand for his, and shook it hastily.

For want of any better address to give, Elie told the driver to take him to the station.

Strutting on her absurdly high heels, the fur coat drawn tightly around her hips, Sylvie crossed the sidewalk under cover of the big umbrella. A burst of dance music came with the opening door, and shadowy forms could be seen gliding around behind the curtains.

In the brightly lighted entrance Sylvie turned and waved to him. The driver let in the gear. It was cold inside the taxi and, huddled up in his corner without his overcoat, Elie felt as if he had nothing on.

"Station's shut." The driver pointed to the dark entrance in which most of the lights had been turned off.

"That doesn't matter."

A sudden panic came over him; he had just realized that besides the thousand-franc notes he had only some small change. But after hunting in his pockets he scraped together enough to pay the taxi driver.

But it meant that he couldn't spend any more money till next morning. There was nowhere to go, eating and drinking were ruled out—and the night was getting steadily colder.

He was so numb that he had stopped being conscious of the cold. He walked on and on, now and then stopping in a doorway, but always hurrying away the moment he heard footsteps. After a while he noted four big clocks at different points, and kept moving in a circle, figuring out how many rounds he would have made before daybreak. He had only the sound of his own steps for company, but, for all their regularity, they afforded some distraction because the echo varied with the different streets. It depended on the width of the road, the height of the houses, and perhaps on the kind of paving used, as well.

Meanwhile, Sylvie was dancing at the Merryland. He wasn't in the least jealous, though he knew she was having what she regarded as a good time. There was nothing to prevent his lying in wait and watching her come out, but it never occurred to him to do so.

It was a relief when the first streetcar made its appearance, and at seven he chose a taxi from those in the rank at Place de Brouckère.

"Drive me to Charleroi."

He had a three-day growth of beard. The shoulders of his coat were drenched and the bottoms of his trouser legs a limp, shapeless mass. The driver looked him up and down, and hesitated. Finally, in the tone of a man who is chancing it, he said:

"All right. Hop in."

The snow had melted. Fields and forest were black as ink. The whole visible world was saturated with moisture, exuding a cold, dank vapor, and there was nobody to be seen in any of the villages along the road.

"Stop somewhere where I can change a thousand-franc note," said Elie as they entered Charleroi.

It was nearly nine. Shops were open, but the town, like the countryside, seemed plunged in a sort of stupor, like a hibernating animal. The light was greenish-gray, an undersea light, and lights were on in most of the shops.

"Look, you'd better drop me at a barber's."

The barber didn't have change for a thousand-franc note, but he ran out himself to change it at a co-operative store across the way. The taxi drove off. While the barber tucked a towel into his collar, Elie studied his reflected self and noticed that his eyes were bloodshot.

"You're a foreigner, eh? You must do well over the exchange, with our Belgian franc so low. . . . Shall I trim your hair, sir, too?"

Trucks were rumbling past the window. The barber's fingers were stained with nicotine, and the smell of tobacco mingling with that of soap made Elie feel sick.

"We have lots of foreigners in Charleroi, mostly young fellows who come to learn their jobs in the coal mines and factories. But they're all on the rocks, these days, what with the depression . . . A dry shampoo, sir?"

When Elie rose from the barber's chair, he was feeling thoroughly sorry for himself. Instead of improving his appearance, the barber's operations had made him look even more haggard than before. But probably there was something wrong with the mirror. For instance, never until now had he noticed that his nose was crooked. And his upper lip seemed much thinner than the lower one.

"Is it far to Rue du Laveu?"

"A fair piece. You'd better take the Number 3. The streetcar stop's just on the right as you go out."

It was still raining, always the same misty drizzle. The streetcar was empty, but Elie remained on the platform. The conductor gave him the word when they reached Rue du Laveu, and he walked up a street bordered by rows of houses all exactly alike.

In spite of the rain, a woman was outside, washing a doorstep, crouching low, with her back to the street, and Elie saw that the number of the house was 53.

"Excuse me. Can I speak to Madame Baron?"

"I'm Madame Baron."

Holding a scrub brush in her right hand, she took a long look at him.

"It's about the room." He pointed to the sign fixed to the window with strips of tape.

"Please step inside. Would you kindly wait a moment in the kitchen?"

The hall had just been washed; the red-and-yellow tiles were clean and glossy. Three overcoats and a raincoat hung on the bamboo coat stand. Elie knocked on the glass door of the kitchen, and a male voice called: "Come in."

A young man, sitting with his feet in the oven, gazed keenly at the newcomer. At the table sat another student, in blue-striped pajamas, his black hair plastered down with brilliantine. He was spreading a slice of bread and butter with jam.

"Won't you sit down? I suppose you've come about the room for rent?"

Out in the hall, Madame Baron was taking off her clogs and wiping her hands on her apron. Voices could be heard on the upper floor, and Elie was aware of a domestic life in which he had no part, as yet.

"All right. Now we can talk. . . . But imagine coming out without an overcoat in weather like this! You must be perishing!"

"Oh, that's because I left my luggage . . ."

"You're not living in Charleroi?"

"No. I've just come from Brussels."

Automatically she was pouring out a cup of coffee for the visitor.

"Antoinette!" she shouted toward the stairs. "Go and see if the front room's tidy."

She seemed unable to keep still for a moment. While she talked, she busied herself putting coal in the stove, stirring the contents of a saucepan, filling a sugar bowl.

"Monsieur Valesco, didn't I ask you once for all not to come downstairs in your pajamas? A gentleman like you ought to know better. . . . Move back a little, Monsieur Moise. How do you think I can go about my work with your legs stuck in the oven?"

The door opened; Antoinette came in and gave Elie a long stare. She was wearing a black knitted dress—obviously homemade—that revealed the immature lines of her body, rather scraggy shoulders, the timid curve of breasts set very wide apart, unformed hips. Her stockings sagged. The small, freckled face was crowned with a mop of unruly red hair.

Her mother snapped at her:

"Where are your manners? Can't you say 'Good morning' to the gentleman?"

Her only response was a slight, defiant shrug. Then she deliberately sniffed Valesco's hair, remarking:

"I can't stand men who soak themselves in scent, like street girls."

Meanwhile she was continuing to cast curious glances at Elie.

"Would you like to see the room?" her mother asked him. "It's 300 francs a month, coal and electric light extra. Perhaps I'd better tell you this is a quiet house, and I don't allow my lodgers to take young ladies into their bedrooms."

She led the way down the hall and opened the first door on

the left. There was a smell of beeswax. Against the pink-papered wall was a brass bedstead with a red quilt. Suddenly Elie turned quite pale, and felt his head going around. . . . He took a quick step toward the bed.

At seven in the evening, when all the household was beginning to gather in the kitchen, he was still asleep, his mouth open, his hair plastered with sweat upon his forehead.

4

Madame Baron scowled when she saw Domb settling down quite coolly with his cracker box at the place she had laid so carefully.

"That's Monsieur Elie's place."

Domb was a Pole, tall, fair-haired, blue-eyed, and hard-featured. He was always very spick-and-span, and kept a dignified appearance even on such occasions as the present— when he had a battered cracker box under his arm. Rising with deliberate slowness, he inquired stiffly:

"May I ask where you wish me to sit?"

The kitchen was far from large, and much of the available space was taken up by a big cookstove of white and gold enamel. At the end of the table farthest from the stove, next to the sideboard, was the wicker armchair reserved for the head of the household, Monsieur Baron.

The others fitted themselves in as best they could around the table, in the order of their coming, because they didn't wait till everybody was present to begin the evening meal. For one thing, Baron's mealtimes varied from day to day, according to the train on which he was on duty. His wife served him, moving back and forth between the stove and his armchair, sometimes pausing to sit down for a moment and snatch a mouthful herself. Meanwhile, Antoinette, her elbows planted on the table, exchanged back talk with the young men.

That was the procedure in the evening. At midday it was different, for Madame Baron planned the meal, whereas at night the lodgers were expected to fend for themselves. Each of the young men brought a tin box containing bread, a slab of butter, some cheese or ham. Also, each had a personal coffee-pot or teapot.

Domb was scowling at the place where he had so often had his meal. It was bad enough to be evicted from it, but to make things worse, he noticed that the best dinner service, with a pink floral pattern, which was never used on ordinary occasions, had been got out. In the hors d'oeuvre dishes were real hors d'oeuvre: sardines, slices of cold sausage, and small smoked fish.

Even Baron, as he munched hunks of bread after dipping them in his coffee, kept eying with an odd expression this lavish outlay. Noticing this, his wife helped him to three smoked fish.

"Monsieur Elie is taking full board." There was a hint of pride in her voice.

"He's a Jew," muttered Domb, as he put the frying pan on the fire.

"How can you tell? You have Jews on the brain, Monsieur Domb. Anyhow, even if he is, I can't see what difference it makes to you."

Domb was feeling disconsolately inside his cracker box.

"Well, what is it you haven't got this evening?"

"Butter."

"All right. I'll lend you some. But it's the last time, I warn you. You're always short of something or other, and I've had enough of it. Why don't you act like Monsieur Moise?"

He dropped a small piece of butter into the frying pan and broke an egg over it, while Madame Baron went into the hall and shouted:

"Monsieur Moise! We're starting."

As Domb fried his egg he cast sour glances at the meat sizzling in another pan, the potatoes and Brussels sprouts in saucepans—all for the newcomer.

"What's he studying?" he asked as he dropped into a chair beside Antoinette.

"Nothing. He finished his studies years ago."

Moise came in, his fuzzy hair standing up like a shaving brush, his eyes red from poring over his books. He was a Polish Jew, and his mother, a domestic servant in Warsaw, sent him enough each month for his keep, while a charitable institution paid his tuition fees.

Moise, too, stared at the unaccustomed splendor of the table, wondering where he was to sit; there was no question of taking the chair beside Domb, who never addressed him, and, indeed, pretended to be unaware of his presence.

"Sit here, Monsieur Moise," said Madame Baron almost tenderly, for Moise was her special favorite. "I'll bet you let your fire go out again."

She knew he did it for economy's sake. He worked in an overcoat, sometimes with a blanket, as well, wrapped around his shoulders. When he came down, his fingers were always stiff from the cold.

"I've started your tea."

He didn't eat an egg; only bread and butter. Madame Baron, who had a habit of nosing around her lodgers' rooms, was the only one who knew his secret—that he wore no socks.

"I wonder if he's still asleep?" she added, referring to Elie.

"He's a queer bird, anyhow," Domb muttered. "Don't like his looks."

"Can't you mind your own business, instead of talking against other people? Always running people down, that's you, Monsieur Domb. As if the Poles were so much better than everybody else!"

She went out again into the hall and called as naturally as if she had been doing it for weeks:

"Monsieur Elie! Dinner's ready."

Valesco hadn't turned up yet, but that was not surprising; sometimes he did not appear at all for the evening meal. Everyone knew he had a girl friend in Brussels, and, when flush, he took her out to dinner.

"It seems that Monsieur Elie is a Jew, too," sighed Madame Baron.

"A Levantine Jew," Moise amended. "That's not the same thing."

"Why not?"

"Oh, it's hard to explain; but there's a difference."

"Of course he's very dark, and you are really rather fair. . . ."

There were footsteps in the hall, followed by a light tap on the kitchen door. Elie came in, and hesitated, blinking at the light and the already overcrowded table.

"You've met my lodgers, haven't you? Let me introduce my husband, who works for the state railway."

Baron rose, held out his hand punctiliously, and tugged at his long gray mustache. He was collarless, and a brass-capped stud glinted in the neckband of his shirt.

"Sit down, Monsieur Elie. You must be dreadfully hungry. You haven't had a bite since this morning."

He sat down at the end of the table, facing Baron, taking that seat as if it fell to him by right. Domb looked away deliberately; while Antoinette seemed fascinated by the dark rings around the newcomer's eyes. Moise said to him, but without much show of interest:

"You're from Istanbul, aren't you?"

"Well, my parents are Portuguese. But I was born in Istanbul. . . . You're a Pole, eh?"

"*I* am a Pole," Domb broke in, straightening up as if his national anthem were being played.

Valesco hurried in, bringing a waft of scent and cold air into the overheated room.

"Am I late?"

"You're always late."

He stopped short, seeing the new lodger in the best place, with the array of hors d'oeuvre in front of him. After a sniff directed at the meat sizzling on the stove, he looked inquiringly at Antoinette.

But she vouchsafed no explanation, while her mother pointed to an empty chair.

"Hurry up and start your dinner."

The walls were white enamel, and what with the glare and the heat Elie felt slightly dizzy. Moise's tin box touched his hors d'oeuvre dish, and the young men were packed so tightly around the table that they jogged each other's elbows. Domb had to move his chair alongside Madame Baron's to make room for Valesco.

The Rumanian had fished out of his pocket a package containing some small pork pies; he got more money from his people than the others, and whenever he ran short, always managed to get a loan.

"Do you know Rumania?" he asked Elie.

"Yes. I once spent a year in Bucharest."

"Fine city, isn't it? And Constanta! What a glorious climate! It's a bit of a change living in a hole like this, where one wallows in mud from one year's end to the other."

"Then why do you stay here?" Madame Baron retorted.

"No offense meant . . . But ask Monsieur Nagear. Just ask him if there's any other country that can touch Rumania. And living's dirt cheap there; why, a chicken costs only a few cents!"

The blood had risen to Elie's head, and the clatter of knives and forks, the buzz of voices, confused him. It was impossible for him to move an inch without touching Moise on his left or Valesco on his right. His mind seemed to have gone blank, and he gazed with unseeing eyes at the people around the table, the tin boxes, the cups of coffee, as he went on eating, almost unconsciously, his meat and vegetables. Suddenly he heard Madame Baron's voice directed toward him.

"What do you drink with your meals?" she asked.

"In my country we always have raki. I don't suppose you know it. . . . I'll have water, please."

He had no appetite. His nose felt hot and swollen, and there was a throbbing in his temples, as if he were immersed in an overhot bath. Baron, who had finished his meal, pushed back his chair and opened an evening paper.

Each of these people lived for himself or herself; the Barons no less than those birds of passage, their lodgers. While old Baron puffed at a big meerschaum pipe and read his paper, Antoinette began washing up on a corner of the stove.

Elie wasn't thinking of Van der Boomp, or even of Sylvie—though it was in this house she had spent her childhood. All sorts of vague ideas were drifting through his mind. That he was older than the other lodgers; that, because he was paying for full board, he'd be treated with special consideration. This last thought gave him pleasure.

"Do you like cheese to finish off with?"

"Yes, but I don't feel hungry tonight."

He had given his landlady 1,000 francs, one of the notes from the wad, though the monthly rate was only 800 francs.

"You can carry forward the difference," he had said.

He had glimpses of the newspaper, the *Gazette de Charleroi*, a local daily printed on spongy paper in exceedingly large type.

As usual, Madame Baron was on her feet most of the time, occasionally stopping to eat a few mouthfuls. It was she who waited on Elie.

"Won't you finish your meat?"

"Sorry, but this awful cold I have seems to have killed my appetite."

Baron looked up from his paper.

"An influenza epidemic is raging all over Europe," he announced. "I see that the death rate in London went up thirty percent last week."

He had a slow, oracular way of speaking. Each time he puffed out the pipe smoke his long mustache streamed forward from his lips.

"Have they caught the murderer yet?" Antoinette asked.

Though he knew this referred to him, Elie didn't turn a hair, and looked up with no more show of interest than the others.

"No, not yet. But the police are on his tracks, it seems, and an early arrest may be expected. They've made inquiries at Van der Cruyssen's bank and got the numbers of the banknotes."

Baron looked around the room, and a change came over his face; he became the vigilant employee of the Belgian state railway, whose duty it was to go from car to car checking tickets.

"And to think there's some people say there aren't any risks in our job!" he exclaimed. "Why, that fellow might easily have killed the conductor as well!"

He seemed put out by the faint smile, quickly repressed, that rose to Elie's lips.

"Aye, it's a dangerous job, whatever you may think. And in spite of that, they've put our retiring age back to sixty, just like the fellows who work in the office. It ain't fair."

Elie's smile had been no more than a nervous reflex. While Baron was speaking, he had been observing Madame Baron, and had noticed a slight change in her expression, as if a vague suspicion—less than that; an unformulated thought—had crossed her mind. And he had guessed its cause: that reference to the banknotes. The thousand-franc note he had given her must be still in the house.

"Some coffee?"

He had used only two notes so far: the one that the barber had changed at the co-operative store, and the one given to Madame Baron, which, after folding it several times, she had slipped into her purse.

"No, thanks. I never drink coffee at night."

"Do you know how many marks of blows were found on the corpse? Eighteen!"

He was as amazed as the others.

"Yes, eighteen blows with a wrench. They think the murderer must be a garage mechanic or something of that sort; anyhow, someone who's used to handling tools. The police officer who checked the passports doesn't remember the nationality of the man in the compartment with the Dutchman, because there were a number of foreigners on the train. But he believes the man was an Italian, or a Greek."

Madame Baron was taking from the oven the custard she had made for Elie. The others had finished their meal. Domb, who had been particularly taciturn all evening, banged the lid on his tin box, rose, and stalked out, after making a gesture like a military salute.

"He's furious," Valesco remarked to Elie.

"Why?"

"Because you're a newcomer, and you're better off than he. Also because you're a Jew, and he loathes Jews."

"He should have more sense," Madame Baron observed severely; she was washing the plates her daughter handed her. "What's the point of loathing people if they don't do you no harm. Before the war I had a Russian and a Pole here. Well, those two young men stayed two years under this roof without even saying 'Good morning' to each other. I never heard such nonsense! . . . Antoinette, give Monsieur Elie an ashtray."

Baron went on reading. His pipe was sizzling. Elie felt a warm, agreeable languor coming over him as, resting his elbows on the table, he smoked a cigarette. He could feel the

51

blood coursing through his veins, a tingling in his nose and throat, and the tobacco had a queer, spicy flavor.

There was a clatter of dishes from the small zinc basin in which the two women were washing up. Moise was staring at the tablecloth, while Valesco smoked a Turkish cigarette that Elie had given him.

"We dine much later in Istanbul."

"Oh? What time?"

"Nine or ten."

"What do you have to eat?" asked Madame Baron.

"We start off with all sorts of tasty little items that we call *mazet*. After that comes lamb and vegetables—perhaps half a dozen kinds of vegetables—and fruit to finish up with."

"Are they good cooks in your part of the world?"

"First-rate!"

He recalled that last evening at Abdullah with his friends; the sideboard heaped with succulent fare of all descriptions.

"Stuffed vine leaves, for instance," he murmured.

"Well, I never! I'm not so sure I'd like that. Stuffed vine leaves—they *must* taste funny!"

At Abdullah he had had an almost royal send-off, and everyone had said to him when he announced that he was leaving: "Lucky devil!"

"What language do you speak at home?"

"French."

"Don't you have another language?"

"Yes, there's Turkish, of course. But all the better-class people speak French among themselves."

"Imagine that!"

Antoinette was watching him from the corner of an eye. She seemed to be trying to size him up but she couldn't manage it—and this annoyed her.

"At Pera everybody's out till late at night." There was an undertone of regret in Elie's voice. "One meets one's friends and roams around the streets, dropping into little cafés, where they have orchestras and singers. You can't imagine how mild and pleasant the night air is in Turkey. Nobody dreams of going to bed before midnight."

"Just like Rumania," Valesco put in approvingly. "You'll see as many people in the streets at midnight as at six in the evening."

"That's all very fine," said Madame Baron, "but what about going to work next morning?"

Elie blew his nose again, and she remarked compassionately:

"Why, your handkerchief's wet through! I'll lend you one to keep you going till your things come. . . . Antoinette, go and get one of your dad's hankies, the ones in the left-hand drawer."

Elie was thinking of the two banknotes, the one at the co-operative store, and the other, in his landlady's purse. He wasn't really anxious. Still, he proposed, as soon as Baron had finished with his paper, to ask him for the loan of it and, if the numbers of the stolen notes were there, to burn it in his bedroom fire. As for the co-operative, they weren't likely to check the numbers on the hundreds of notes they must receive each day.

"Do you come from Vilna itself?" he asked Moise.

"Yes. I've always lived there."

"I've been there twice, both times in the winter. It seemed pretty grim."

"Ah, but you should see it in the summer."

"What subject are your studying?"

"Chemistry. I've finished the course. But I'm staying on an extra year to study glass-making."

Moise addressed him in a tone in which deference mingled with rancor; the tone a ghetto-born Polish Jew employs when speaking to an emancipated Jew from southern Europe.

"In the Stop Press news," Baron announced, after taking a pull at his pipe," they say the murderer seems to have had an accomplice—a man or a woman, they aren't sure which. Madame Van der Cruyssen is now in Paris and is making arrangements to have the body moved there."

"Oh, he was married?"

For a moment Elie gasped. He'd never thought of that! Then he started trying to picture what the Dutchman's wife might look like.

"There's her photo."

It was badly reproduced, all in smudgy grays, but one could distinctly see a very tall, stately looking lady trying to elude the photographer's camera.

"She looks much younger than he," Elie remarked.

The photograph gave the impression of a woman in her middle thirties. She had not had time to procure full mourning. Antoinette came back.

"Here's a handkerchief."

Elie took the opportunity to blow his nose lengthily; when he put the handkerchief in his pocket, his face was scarlet. Noticing this, Madame Baron waxed motherly again.

"Listen! I'll make you a nice hot toddy, and you'd better take two aspirin before going to bed."

"Thanks very much. Sorry to give you all this trouble . . ."

"Oh, I'm used to it. You young fellows never know how to look after yourselves."

It was amusing to be treated as a "young fellow" like the others, when he was thirty-five! Thirty-five—that must be about Madame Van der Cruyssen's age. . . .

Moise got up, muttering a vague "Good night," and went off to his room. Madame Baron listened to the receding footsteps, then quietly closed the door.

"He's another," she sighed. "Just now I told him to finish the meat you didn't eat. But he was too proud. And all the poor boy has to eat is an egg a day, and some bread and butter."

"Why couldn't he have stayed in his country," Valesco said rather peevishly, "instead of coming here to study?"

"What about *you*?"

"That's quite different. My people can afford to see I have enough."

"One wouldn't think so—not at the end of the month, anyhow. You're always just as short of cash as he, the last ten days."

She went on washing up as she talked, saying the first thing that came into her head, with a sort of rough good humor. Meanwhile, Baron had started a new page of his newspaper. Antoinette, who was putting back the cups and plates in a cupboard behind her father, gave a push to his armchair.

"Want me to move?" he grunted.

"Don't bother. I've almost done."

Madame Baron tipped the dirty water out into the sink, and wrung out the dishcloth with a brisk turn of her wrists. Valesco rose, stretched himself, and yawned.

"Surely you're not going out at this hour?" Madame Baron exclaimed.

"Got to, I'm afraid."

"Now look here, if you make any noise coming in, or forget the key again, I warn you straight, you won't stay here another hour. I have no use for men who are always running after . . . after women who're no better than they should be."

Valesco winked at Elie, who was lighting another cigarette. Now that the room was quieter, the ticking of the alarm clock standing on the mantelpiece between two brass candlesticks could be heard now and again.

"Good night, Antoinette. Good night, everyone."

And Valesco retired to his room to powder his face, brush his hair, and spray some more scent on it before going out.

"They're only youngsters," Madame Baron confided to Elie, "and if I didn't scold them now and then, there'd be no peace in the house. Of course, I saw at once you were different, a quiet sort of fellow. Still, I can't understand a sensible man like you getting mixed up in politics. It don't seem natural."

When asking her not to report his presence to the police, he had told her he'd been banished from his country because of his political activities.

"Who's the big man in Turkey? A king? A president?"

"Neither. A dictator."

He smiled. He was aching in every limb, but, strangely enough, the sensation was more agreeable than otherwise— almost voluptuous. The warmth and intimacy of this humble little kitchen were acting like an anodyne on his jaded nerves.

Now and again he caught Antoinette gazing at him in a curiously rapt manner, and this added to his satisfaction; there was no doubt he'd made a strong impression on her. Not altogether a favorable impression, judging by what he saw in her eyes. It was more like a vague mistrust; as if she, unlike the others, was intelligent enough to realize he had no business in such a house as this. But it proved one thing, anyhow: that she was definitely interested in him—perhaps afraid of becoming too much interested.

He couldn't bring himself to move. The table had been cleared and spread with a blue-and-white-checked oilcloth. Seated beside the stove, Madame Baron was peeling potatoes for the next day's meals, while Antoinette darned socks, Domb's or Valesco's probably.

"I can't abide people who turn up their noses at everybody else, as if they were the lords of creation," Madame Baron remarked. "Most of the Poles I have here are like that." She turned to her husband. "Germain, why don't you offer Monsieur Elie a little drink?"

He jumped up hastily and took a bottle of sloe gin from the cupboard.

"Tell me what you think of it. It comes from Luxembourg. I'm on duty on the train there once a week."

The liqueur gave off a heady fragrance. The smell of pipe smoke mingled in the air with the subtler smell of Turkish cigarettes. Now and again they heard Valesco's footsteps in the room above.

"He sometimes works thirteen or fourteen hours a day. He has a letter from his mother once a week, and, would you believe it, she has to get a neighbor to write it for her! Imagine there being folk in these days who don't know how to write!"

The good lady seemed capable of rambling on like this for hours, but Elie had no wish to stop her. He was actually getting to enjoy his cold, and derived a faint, recurrent thrill of pleasure from the twinges in his neck.

He pictured the scene in the street outside, the black, shabby houses, a squalid sky hung low above the dripping roofs, the air throbbing with a dark clangor of machinery. Here, in this cozy little kitchen, all that seemed infinitely remote, less real than a dream.

"Well, what do you think of it?" Baron took a sip of the liqueur, then wiped his mustache with the back of his hand. "You've nothing like this in your country, eh?"

"No, but, as I told you, we have raki. It's an excellent liqueur, rather like what they drink in Egypt and Bulgaria."

"Been there, too?"

"Yes, I've been pretty well all over Europe. My father was an exporter of Turkish tobacco."

"Like Monsieur Weiser," Madame Baron commented, for her husband's benefit. She uttered the name in a respectful tone.

It was ten past ten. Now and then Antoinette would toss her head back when a lock of red hair straggled across her eyes. . . . Baron was the first to yawn. Then he folded his paper and put it on the table.

"May I have a look at it?"

"By all means. Afraid you won't find much to interest you, though. It's mostly local news. The glass workers are threatening to go on strike. . . . Won't you have another glass?"

And Elie, his cheeks deeply flushed and eyes fever-bright, his nose swollen to twice its normal size, felt himself sinking still deeper into a pleasant coma of no thoughts.

"What are you dreaming about, Antoinette? Why don't you go and make Monsieur Elie's bed?"

They could hear her turning the mattress, patting the eiderdown, drawing tight the sheets.

"Sleep well. And don't be in a hurry to get up tomorrow. Once you're in bed, I'll bring you a hot drink and some aspirin."

Only one thing was preying on his mind as he undressed in the unfamiliar room: the picture of Van der Cruyssen's wife. Poor as the reproduction was, it gave a definite impression of quiet beauty; to Elie's thinking, she was much too refined-looking, and, above all, far too young, to be the wife of that fat, elderly Dutchman.

There was a knock on the door.

"Are you in bed?" Madame Baron asked.

"Just a moment. . . . All right. Come in now."

Still holding the tray, she stooped to pick up the trousers he had let fall on the floor, and to place them on a chair.

"It's nice and hot," she said in an almost motherly tone. "Drink it right away, young man, and you'll feel ever so much better in the morning."

5

Sylvie got off at the streetcar stop in front of the grocery, three doors from her mother's house. For a moment, as he picked her way across the puddles, she wondered if Madame Horisse, who owned the grocery and was always watching at her window, would recognize her.

The door was ajar and she had no need to knock. She pushed it open, took two steps forward, and saw her mother in the front room, and noticed that the bed had been slept in.

"Oh, it's you, Sylvie. You gave me quite a turn. Why didn't you say 'Good morning'?" By force of habit Madame Baron proffered her cheek to be kissed, and Sylvie brushed it with her lips. A bottle of rum, with an empty glass beside it, stood on the bedside table.

"Going to stay here for a while, or is it one of your flying visits?"

There was always a vaguely suspicious look in Madame Baron's eyes when she observed her daughter, and now nothing escaped her; neither the fact that she had a new handbag and a new, rather austerely cut tailor-made outfit, nor that her eyes had dark rings around them and she seemed worried about something.

"I'll go and have a cup of coffee in the kitchen," Sylvie said abruptly.

She felt sure this was Elie's bedroom, but dared not ask her mother. The kitchen, when she entered it, was full of steam, and a man was sitting in front of the stove. The air was so thick that she almost collided with him.

"Can't you see the soup's boiling over?" she exclaimed, and shifted the saucepan to the edge of the stove.

The circle of glowing coal came into view, and Sylvie began hunting for the lid of the saucepan. When she turned, she saw Moise on his feet, bowing to her. He was holding some mimeographed sheets, evidently from a course he was studying.

Elie, who was at the table, eating eggs and bacon, rose slightly from his seat.

"Go on with your breakfast. Don't mind me!"

The window was coated with vapor, even the walls were wet, and the atmosphere was so stifling that Sylvie went to the door and opened it a few inches, meanwhile casting furtive glances at Elie.

He had only just got up, and all he had done to make himself presentable was to run a comb through his hair. Like Baron on his return from work, he was in his shirt sleeves.

He went on eating, taking no notice of Sylvie, and Moise settled down again to his studies. One had the impression of a family scene that had been momentarily interrupted—so rooted did the two men seem in their surroundings.

Seating herself in the wicker armchair, Sylvie asked:

"Got a cold?"

"Yes, I have a beastly cold. And a stiff neck, too."

She gazed at him intently. A silence followed, so tense with unspoken thoughts that the student looked up uneasily from his papers and stared first at Sylvie, then at Nagear. Sylvie was the first to speak.

"Are you comfortable here?"

"Very comfortable indeed. Everyone's most kind."

And now Sylvie's lips tightened; she made no effort to conceal her ill humor. She was raging, perhaps against Elie, perhaps against the tiresome young student who persisted in staying where he wasn't wanted.

"I wonder that Mother stands it, having the lodgers cluttering up the kitchen all the time."

Quietly Moise rose, went to the door, and vanished up the hall. Sylvie decided not to waste a moment. Bending forward, she said in a low tone:

"They've found out the numbers of the notes."

"I know that."

There was a flash of anger in her eyes.

"You know that—and you can sit here calmly, eating your breakfast!"

That was so; he felt quite calm. He hadn't realized it at first, but, now that she pointed it out, he was amazed at his tranquillity. He had sweated copiously all night and his cold was much better. Only his stiff neck was still giving trouble; he had to be careful how he moved his head.

"Did you pay my mother in advance?"

"Of course."

She shot a sharp glance at him, then rose and opened the soup tureen on the sideboard. It was never used for soup, and served as a receptacle for odds and ends. In it now were some old letters, a tax receipt, a little silver bell with a blue tassel. There was also Madame Baron's purse, and in it Sylvie found the thousand-franc note.

"Well, what are you going to do about it?"

From this time on it was clear that they no longer understood each other. Indeed, there were moments when Elie seemed to have no idea to what she was referring. After a pause he answered gloomily:

"Surely it's obvious there's nothing to be done."

She replaced the lid on the soup tureen.

"Anyhow, you've got to put another note instead of that one in Mother's purse. . . . Do you hear?"

She was talking much too loudly; losing her head, in fact. Elie put a warning finger to his lips and, to keep himself calm, fell to poking the fire, as he'd seen Moise doing earlier in the morning.

"I've brought your luggage. It's at the station café."

Elie poured himself another cup of coffee, then looked at Sylvie as if to ask, "Would you like some, too?"

Just then she noticed the brown felt slippers he was wearing —her father's slippers.

"Listen! You can't stay here. One of the railway staff has told the police he saw you coming back to Belgium. They're hunting for you in Brussels."

"Are you still at the Palace?"

"Don't be a damned fool!" she snapped.

She went to the door and, opening it, saw her mother washing the tiles in the hall.

"What! Saturday already!" she exclaimed; then she closed the door, and said to Elie: "If you must know, I'm sharing a room with another girl, one of the Merryland crowd. And I've told her everything. She's a pal of mine."

He was standing in front of the stove, toasting his back, his eyes fixed on the window and the dreary little back yard.

"I suppose you think you're mighty clever, Elie—but I tell you straight: you've got to clear out of here."

He bent his head, like a scolded schoolboy, and said weakly:

"How can I? I don't have any money."

"That's your problem. . . . Wait! Here's 300 francs; that will see you across the Dutch frontier."

His apathy was getting on her nerves.

"Didn't you hear what I said? For God's sake try to wake up!"

"Ssh! Your mother's coming."

That was so. Madame Baron entered, wiping her hands, and again, when she looked at her daughter, a vague suspicion flickered in her eyes.

"Your room's ready, Monsieur Elie. Antoinette will be back in a few minutes, and she'll light your fire. I'll be needing the kitchen soon; I have to wash the floor and scour the saucepans."

She moved the pots on the stove, put some coal on the fire, and bustled out.

No sooner had she gone than Sylvie turned on him.

"The truth is, you haven't the guts to make a move. You'd rather stick here like a limpet."

"Three hundred francs wouldn't see me far. And, anyhow, I don't see what harm I do by staying here."

He winced; without thinking, he had just turned his head too quickly. Never before had Sylvie seen him in this state, his clothes bedraggled, his collar stud jogging on his Adam's apple, his feet in shabby slippers much too large for him. What was more, he seemed to take a certain pleasure in flaunting his abasement.

"At any rate, you've burned the other notes, haven't you?"

"Not yet. How about you?"

"I've burned mine."

He knew that she was lying.

"Oh, there's Antoinette coming back!"

Already he could recognize her footsteps. She rattled the mail slot, and her mother opened the door. A minute later she came into the kitchen, and stopped short on seeing her sister there.

"So, you're here. . . ."

She had been to the butcher's. After slamming some meat

63

down on the table she held up her cheek toward Sylvie to be kissed, as her mother had done; then she went to the fire and warmed her hands. No one spoke for some minutes. Finally, Antoinette gave her sister a frankly disapproving glance, and said sulkily:

"Hope I'm not intruding."

"What's come over you?"

"And look here, when you give me stockings, you might at least bring silk ones! . . . Monsieur Elie, the best thing you can do is to go straight to bed."

She was obviously determined to remain in the kitchen—if only to spite her sister.

"Will you be here for lunch, Sylvie?"

"Don't think so."

"Then why ever did you come? . . . Monsieur Elie, if you *must* stay in the kitchen, you might at least sit down. It makes me quite dizzy seeing you standing up, with your head cocked on one side."

"I see your manners haven't improved," Sylvie remarked.

"Why should they? I ain't a grand lady. I don't wear silk stockings."

A long silence followed. The soup began to simmer again, filling the air with steam.

"I *must* know if you're staying to lunch, because if you are, I'll go out and buy a steak."

"Don't bother."

Antoinette's gaze fell on the soup tureen on the sideboard. After a quick glance at her sister, she walked up to it. She had noticed that the lid had been replaced carelessly, at a slant. Lifting it, she fumbled inside, opened the purse, and seemed reassured.

"What are you doing?" Sylvie asked.

"Oh, nothing. But I might ask *you* that, mightn't I? It's funny you should come all the way from Brussels just to spend a few minutes in a kitchen that stinks of cabbage soup."

Sylvie merely shrugged her shoulders, and said to Elie:
"Give me a cig."

Antoinette kept her eyes fixed on her.

"You'd rather I left you to yourselves, wouldn't you? . . .
All right, I'll go."

The moment her sister had left, Sylvie bent toward him,
asking:

"Have you told her anything?"

"Not likely!"

"Anyhow, get this into your head, Elie: *you've got to go*! . . .
You understand?"

Just then the door opened, and she drew back hastily. Very
spick-and-span, as usual, Domb clicked his heels together
and, stooping, kissed the hand she extended to him.

"I must apologize for entering so abruptly. I'd no idea that I
would find myself in the presence of a charming lady!" He was
a very susceptible young man, and addicted to high-flown
phrases. Turning to Elie, he added: "May I hope you're feeling better after a good night's rest?"

Without seeming to notice the far from cordial expression
on their faces, he held his white, well-kept hands toward the
fire, rubbing them together.

"If I'm not mistaken, this is the second time I've had the
pleasure of seeing you, Mademoiselle, and as I said yesterday
to your mother . . ."

"That reminds me, I've something to tell her," Sylvie interrupted, and hurried out of the kitchen.

"What on earth's the matter with her?" Domb looked quite
startled. "Did I say something I shouldn't have?"

Elie gazed at him vaguely, as if he had not heard, and
watched the smoke of his cigarette curling up through the hot,
stagnant air.

Madame Baron was raising her voice in the hall.

"All right, my fine lady, go if you want to, since your home ain't grand enough for you. Sorry we can't offer you chicken and champagne for lunch. . . ."

Sylvie's high heels clicked on the tiled floor. She came back to the kitchen for her bag and snatched it off the table.

"Off already? What a pity!" Domb got into position to kiss her hand again.

She took no notice of him, but, after a venomous glance at Elie, marched out of the kitchen. A moment later the street door banged.

"What a charming, charming girl!" the Pole exclaimed enthusiastically. "I wonder if you realize how . . ."

But, without waiting for him to finish, Elie, too, went out of the room. Antoinette was kneeling in front of the little old-fashioned stove, waiting for the wood to catch before putting on the coal.

The window overlooked the street. The sidewalks were almost dry, but the road was still deep in grimy slush, coated here and there with ice.

Sylvie wasn't to be seen at the streetcar stop outside the grocery, and Elie pictured her stalking angrily toward the center of town. To his left he heard a sound of shrill voices, running feet, and a band of schoolchildren came scampering by. It was half past eleven, and they had just left the schoolhouse at the end of the street.

"By the way," he said to Antoinette, "there's something I'd like to ask you to do."

He waited for some moments, expecting her to look around, but she remained kneeling in front of the stove, without moving. Then, when he least expected it, he heard her ask impatiently:

"Well? What is it?"

"I don't feel up to going out yet. I wonder if you'd be kind enough to go and fetch my luggage?"

"Oh! So you really have some luggage?"

He felt so uncomfortable that he turned his head and looked out the window again.

"I left it at the station café," he said, "since I wasn't sure if I could find a room."

"Why didn't you get Sylvie to bring it? Considering that you sleep with her . . . Oh, it's no use putting on that innocent air, as if butter wouldn't melt in your mouth. Mother's easy game, I know—but you can't fool *me*!" She stopped talking, because the coal was rattling off the shovel into the stove.

When she had finished with the fire, she looked around and saw Elie still gazing out the window.

"Why did my sister come today? . . . No, you don't need to tell me; I can guess. She was in a state because they've got the numbers of the banknotes. It was that, wasn't it? You may as well own up."

Elie went to the door to make sure no one was listening outside. The bed had been made, the room was tidy, and waves of heat were flooding in from the stove, which was roaring cheerfully, red cinders clattering down into the tin tray below.

"Oh, you needn't look so worried; I won't give you away. You know, I guessed at once why you and Sylvie were glaring at each other when I came into the kitchen. Sylvie had been telling you to leave this house. That's right, isn't it?"

At that, he had to turn and face the girl. Her eyes were fixed on him, and in them he could see faint glints of red, like the red of her unruly hair.

"I know my sister much better than you do. You needn't worry about that note in Mother's purse; I'll manage to change it before Monday. First thing this morning I burned the paper that had the numbers in it."

So that was why he hadn't been able to find it! When for a few minutes he had had the kitchen to himself, he'd hunted for it high and low, for he felt fairly sure the newspapers wouldn't publish the numbers of the stolen notes a second time.

"Is your luggage heavy?"

"There are two suitcases and a small bag. You'll need a taxi."

"Just imagine a man like you letting my sister lead him by the nose!"

He vainly tried not to blush.

"All right, I'll go and get your things. Then you'll be able to get into some clean clothes—and high time, too! You look a sight and a fright got up like that!"

He heard her talking to her mother on the landing, then going up another flight of steps. Elie had worked out the number of rooms. Besides his bedroom and the kitchen, the only other room on the ground floor was the dining room, redolent of beeswax, in which no one ever set foot. On the floor above were only two rooms: that of Valesco, immediately overhead, and Domb's at the back, overlooking the yard.

Strictly speaking, there was no third floor. Moise Kaler had an attic room with a dormer window. The Barons occupied another attic room, while their young daughter was relegated to a sort of loft, lighted by a small skylight in the roof.

She went up to it now, to dress. When she came down, she walked through the hall without stopping. Elie saw her going down the street, a thin, childish figure wrapped in a shoddy, ill-fitting green coat.

He noticed that she had a way of pulling her hat absurdly low over her eyes and swaying her meager hips; indeed, anyone who didn't know her might easily have taken her for a juvenile streetwalker on the prowl. Her shoes needed heeling and her stockings were creased. She had been lavish with her lipstick, and her mouth showed as a red gash in her heavily powdered face.

A knock at the door. Madame Baron entered.

"I've come to see if the fire has caught."

She could not stay quiet for five minutes. The stove was so

hot that she had to wrap her hand in her apron before opening the door.

"I'm sure you can't get coal as good as this in your country. I have it direct from the colliery, so it only costs you one franc fifty the scuttle. And Monsieur Domb, who feels the cold terribly, makes a scuttle last two full days, even when it's freezing outside."

She gave a glance around the room to see that all was in order.

"What do you think of my daughter—my eldest, I mean? You mustn't judge her by her looks; she's quite a good girl at heart. Only she's always been crazy about dancing. Still, I confess I wouldn't care to see her here too often. . . . Have you any sisters?"

Elie had to think. He'd almost forgotten if he had any sisters! The question jerked him back into another life, which now seemed infinitely remote. After some moments he said:

"Yes, I have a sister."

"Is she nice-looking? Does she live in Turkey?"

Yes, she lived at Pera. Presumably she was pretty, since all his male friends had shown an interest in her. All the same, though she was twenty-seven, she had never even been engaged. For the first time Elie caught himself wondering if she'd ever had a serious love affair.

With an effort he conjured up a picture of the modernistic apartment in a big block of buildings where Esther and her mother lived. But he found it impossible to visualize the details, and it suddenly struck him that he had never troubled to observe them, and, what surprised him still more, that his sister was a stranger to him.

"Have you any photos in your luggage?"

"No, I don't think I have."

"I'm sorry about that. All my lodgers have pictures of their families hanging in their rooms. So I get to know what their mothers and brothers and sisters look like. Sometimes one of them has his mother come to see him, and she writes to me regular after she's gone back home, and I like that. Last year Monsieur Domb's mother paid him a visit—such a nice lady she is. You'd never think he was her son. He's going bald— you must have noticed that. His mother's such a pretty woman, and quite young. When they're out together you'd take 'em for a pair of lovebirds. It was this room she slept in."

Though she never stopped talking, Madame Baron was always busy doing something, flicking off dust, putting each object in its place. Twice she stepped back to make sure the brass flowerpot holder, standing on a small lace mat, was plumb in the middle of the windowsill.

"I've been meaning to tell you: don't let my husband know I didn't make you fill in the form reporting your arrival to the police. You see, he's in government service himself, and he don't see things like we do."

Now and again a red-and-yellow streetcar clanged past the window. A string of a dozen tipcarts, laden with coal, went slowly by, the big iron wheels grinding on the cobbles, the cartmen walking in front of their horses, whips resting on their shoulders.

Sylvie had to wait till one o'clock for the next train back to Brussels. Sitting in the railway waiting room, she had a glimpse of her sister entering the station café and coming out with Elie's suitcases.

In Brussels, too, it was raining, but the effect was less depressing, what with the shops all lighted up and bursts of music coming from the big cafés.

At eight o'clock Sylvie, already dressed for evening, was sitting by herself near the bandstand in a brasserie, having a meal of cold meat and beer. The pianist, a thin young man, kept smiling at her, and, without thinking, she returned his smile.

It was as restful as a warm bath—this huge room hazy with smoke, full of the fumes of coffee and beer, where the chink of plates and glasses blended with the languorous strains of a Viennese waltz. At a table facing her was a pale, shy-looking youngster, who, cold as the weather was, had only a light rain-coat over his suit. Sylvie observed that he was wearing a flow-ing bow tie and there was a wide-brimmed hat of the "Latin Quarter" type on the chair beside him, which made her smile.

An artist obviously; a painter, or a poet. He couldn't be more than twenty. He was doggedly smoking a small, stumpy pipe and, unlike the pianist, gazing at Sylvie with romantically wistful eyes.

The pianist noticed him as the band was striking up again after a break, and favored Sylvie with a humorous, compre-hending wink.

Time passed slowly. The Merryland did not open till ten. The entertainment manager, who was an acquaintance of Sylvie's, had taken her on as one of his show girls, promising her a solo dance the following week.

There was a constant stir of people coming and going. Games of cards and backgammon were in progress on the marble-topped tables. The layer of smoke between the players' heads and the gilt-scrolled ceiling was steadily growing denser.

At quarter of ten Sylvie left, after bestowing a final smile on the musician. Just before opening the door she chanced to look around and saw that the young man with the Latin Quar-ter hat was following her.

It was raining less heavily. The Merryland was only 500 yards up the street, so she decided to go on foot.

"Wonder if he'll speak to me."

She quickened her pace, slowed down, then hurried on again. When she reached the entrance of the cabaret, the young man hadn't yet accosted her.

"Has Jacqueline come?" she asked the doorman.

"I haven't seen her going in."

She went up to the second floor, left her fur in the cloak-room, and spent some minutes in the Ladies, redoing her make-up. As she walked toward the bar, she saw the young man, perched on a high stool, smoking his pipe and staring with affected ease at the empty room. Just then Jacqueline came in. She was a plump, good-humored young woman in a low-cut green silk dress with a vast pink velvet rose on one shoulder.

"What luck?" asked Sylvie.

The bartender, busy with his bottles and glasses, paid no attention to the two girls.

"I've done Ghent and Antwerp, and managed to change twenty notes. The money's in my bag. . . . What news your end? Have you seen him? How did he strike you?"

"He's a queer bird, and no mistake. He's so calm you wouldn't think he'd done it."

"Will he be coming to Brussels?"

"I wouldn't think so. He seems to have dug himself in there; he just sits in front of the fire, and eats his meals, and . . ."

She stopped speaking. She had noticed the young man gazing hard at her over Jacqueline's shoulder. On the point of making a face at him, for some reason she changed her mind and smiled.

"Barman, the same again," he said.

You could see he wasn't used to it. He'd read that phrase in a novel, most likely. And, though he tried to prevent himself from doing so, when ordering the drink he eyed the price list on the bar, with obvious apprehension.

"What are you going to do, Sylvie?"

"Ask me another! It's no use making plans till we see how things are going to pan out. Anyhow, tomorrow you'd better go and change the other notes in Liège and Namur."

"Do you think it's safe? To tell the truth, I'm beginning to get scared. . . ."

But Jacqueline was amenable; finally she agreed to do whatever Sylvie wanted. A bell tinkled; the first customers of the night were arriving. The two girls gave hasty glances at their faces in the mirror behind the bar, then swung themselves onto stools. The young man's eyes still hung on Sylvie, wistfully imploring.

6

It was the third night. The meal had just ended and the young men were talking at the top of their voices when Elie, who had watched Domb lighting a cigarette, took advantage of a lull to remark:

"I suppose you think that tobacco you're smoking comes from Egypt?"

"Of course it does. I suppose you're going to tell us that it comes from Turkey." Domb had no use for chauvinism—in others.

"That's just where it does come from. For one thing, there's a law forbidding tobacco-growing in Egypt. I've lived there, so I ought to know, and, what's more, my father was one of the leading exporters of oriental tobaccos."

Domb held his peace, and stared moodily at his plate. It was the third meal during which most of the conversation had turned on Turkey, and he preferred not to give Elie another opportunity of showing off.

But Madame Baron, who had an inquiring mind, asked from the end of the table:

"Didn't you take over your father's business?"

"At the time when I could have done so, I was all out for a good time. Traveling about the world. I used to spend the summer in the mountains, in the Tyrol or the Caucasus, and winter in the Crimea or on the Riviera."

"You're an only child, aren't you?"

"No. I've a sister."

"Silly of me to ask! I remember now; you told me you had a sister. Is your father dead?"

"He lost nearly all his money speculating, and I rather think that killed him. When he died, my mother and sister had just enough to live on."

Moise was gazing dreamily at the tablecloth, unaware, to all appearance, that anyone was talking. Now and again Valesco shot a quick, searching glance at Elie. It was Madame Baron, most of all, who seemed to drink in his words, while Antoinette, like Domb, feigned complete indifference.

Baron had already pushed back his chair and started reading the paper. A sharp frost had set in, and children had made slides along the gutters; the night was clear, the sky bathed in a pale, wintry sheen.

"You ought to go out for a bit, Monsieur Elie," Madame Baron had kept telling him. "If you wrap yourself up well, you won't come to any harm. You'll never get well if you stay indoors all the time."

But, though he was blowing his nose less often and was only conscious of his stiff neck now and then—when, for instance, he had been crouching over the fire for an hour or two and suddenly stood up—he hated the idea of going out. He found a curious sensation of well-being within the four walls of this little house, and, though he did absolutely nothing all day, never felt bored. Even the effort of getting fully dressed was too much for him, and he pottered around the house in slippers, collarless, like Baron, the brass cap of his collar stud jogging his Adam's apple.

"So you haven't a photo of your sister with you?"

"No. But I wish I'd brought my pictures; I'd have shown you one of our villa at Prinkipo."

"Prinkipo? Where's that?"

"It's an island in the Sea of Marmara, an hour's ride from Istanbul. In early spring everybody who can manage it clears out of town and goes to Prinkipo, where the climate's simply marvelous. Everyone has his private caïque."

"What's that?"

"A light rowboat, with a sail as well. In the evenings you see dozens of them gliding about on a sea that's calm as a lake. Usually there are musicians on board, and the air is full of music, and the most wonderful scents. The islands are a mass of flowers, and in the distance you see the white minarets tapering up along the coast."

All this was true, and he visualized the scene so clearly that he could have made an accurate sketch of it. And yet somehow he didn't *feel* it. He could hardly convince himself that he had spent a good part of his life there.

That was why he talked about it; and also because he saw Madame Baron drinking it all in. When Antoinette began to show signs of restlessness, her mother turned on her.

"Can't you keep still when Monsieur Elie's speaking?"

His descriptions of the Near East had much the same effect on her as the voices of crooners on the radio; they plunged her into a world where all was glamour.

"Tell me, Monsieur Elie, what sort of clothes do you wear in Turkey?"

"Oh, the same as here. But, before Kemal's rise to power, most people wore oriental dress."

"Did *you*?"

"No. I'm not a Muslim. And, anyhow, the better-class people in Pera always dressed just as they do in Paris—except that one sometimes wore a fez."

Domb, who was looking more and more bored, stood up,

and after a curt bow to the company retired to his room. Madame Baron was so absorbed that she forgot to start washing up, and even Baron now and again looked up from his paper to listen to Elie.

"Of course, life in Pera isn't what it used to be—on account of the depression. But some years ago it was perhaps even more—what shall I call it?—more *brilliant* than in Paris. You could hear every language in the streets, and everyone had pots of money."

That, too, was quite true, yet he had a feeling he was lying. He delved into his memory for something else to tell, something to increase the effect he was already conscious of producing.

"When we went to the seaside, on the Asia Minor coast . . ." he began.

He leaned back in his chair, as he had seen the other lodgers do when the meal was over. When he had finished his description, Madame Baron asked:

"Do your mother and sister know you're in Belgium?"

"No. I haven't written to them yet."

At last Madame Baron had begun washing up, after handing Antoinette a kitchen towel.

"In my country," Valesco said, "Constanta, on the Black Sea, is the great resort. It's quite as stylish as any of the Riviera towns."

But it fell flat. Nobody wanted to hear about Rumania.

"Yes, Constanta's not too bad. But it can't touch the places on the Bosporus!"

Moise, who could have told them only of the Vilna ghetto, went quietly out.

"Why not go to the theater, Monsieur Elie? There's a company from Brussels there tonight. The Number 3 streetcar drops you just at the entrance."

"Thanks for letting me know—but I'd rather stay here."

"What! Don't you like going to the theater?"

"Oh, I'm sick of theaters; been to too many of them, I suppose. One went to a show almost every night, in my country, and was out till three or four in the morning."

There was a homely sound of splashes and the chink of dishes from the basin in which Madame Baron was washing up. Elie was gazing straight in front of him as he puffed at his cigarette, his mind in a pleasant haze, due partly to his cold and partly to the stuffiness of the atmosphere. They seemed to blend so well that he felt no wish to recover, and whenever his fever showed signs of going away he took a gulp of hot toddy to make himself start sweating again.

"Do you intend to stay long in Belgium? I'm sure you must find it dreadfully dull after all the wonderful places you've visited."

What most of all had impressed the good lady was the contents of his suitcases: silk shirts and pajamas embroidered with his initials, a whole repertory of ties, a well-cut tail coat, not to mention a silver toilet set.

Pointing to the tail coat, she had asked:

"Do you wear that often?"

"Whenever I go out at night."

Even he himself had gazed at his evening clothes with a certain wonder. Could it be true that only a fortnight ago he was still on board the *Théophile-Gautier*, one of the little group of Sylvie's admirers, who after dinner always went with her to the smoking room, taking turns to stand champagne all round?

Here there were certain words that acted like a spell, and "champagne" was one of them. He had only to mention it for Madame Baron to conjure up a world of gilded opulence, fantastic orgies. Even such commonplace things as a dress suit and silk pajamas had much the same effect. When he spoke of his mother's maid she asked:

"How many servants did you have?"

"Let's see. . . . Seven all told, including a dear old nurse-maid who was treated like one of the family. And I'm not including our gardeners at Prinkipo, or my sister's governess."

The grotesque thing was that, though every word of this was true, it sounded to him like a fairy tale. And it was also true that his father had died three years previously, after losing practically all his money. Actually, there hadn't been any great change in their life at Pera. His mother had kept on one housemaid and the old nurse at their apartment. The villa at Prinkipo had not been sold, no buyer being forthcoming, and as soon as the weather showed signs of warming up, the two women moved into it each spring.

Had he, Elie, really suffered much by the family debacle? He had behaved just as hundreds of other young Turks had behaved when the depression caught them. In the main street of Pera they were to be seen strolling up and down for hours on end, declaiming poetry, going into the cafés for a drink of raki and a dish of small smoked fish, and, when fortune favored, picking up a girl.

One day he had made 1,000 Turkish pounds by acting as middleman in the sale of an old English freighter to the Greek government. And if the deal in carpets had gone through . . .

"Aren't you going out tonight, Monsieur Valesco?"

"Nothing doing till the first of next month. I'm on the rocks, and I'd rather stay here than go out without a cent in my pocket."

"I know. . . . And when your money comes in, we won't see you in my kitchen in the evening, not even for meals—anyhow, for the first few days."

The washing-up was over, and as usual Madame Baron went to the pantry to get her vegetable basket and a pail. Her husband rose with a sigh and walked to the door. They heard him clumping heavily up the stairs.

"He's on duty on the night train," Madame Baron explained. "He'll be at Herbesthal tomorrow morning, and come back again by the night train. Have you put his clothes out, Antoinette?"

"Yes, Ma. And I sewed on the button."

Valesco, who looked bored, hovered around Elie for some moments, then said:

"Feel like a game of billiards? There's quite a good table at the bistro just up the street."

"No, thanks."

"In that case, I'm off to bed. Good night, everyone."

The only sound in the room was the faint, intermittent squeak of the knife paring the potatoes, and now and again the thud of a potato dropped into the pail.

"It must be nice to travel about the world," said Madame Baron pensively. "I've never had no time to travel, and never will have, I suppose."

Elie saw Antoinette look up sharply, and noticed that her face was pale. Her eyes were fixed on him. She was trying to convey something to him, and was pushing the newspaper in his direction.

"It's in your young days you should travel," Madame Baron continued. She had noticed nothing. Elie took his time before reaching for the newspaper.

A big headline, splashed across three columns, announced that eleven miners had been trapped by a firedamp explosion in the Seraing coal mine. Beside it was a headline in smaller type: THE PARIS EXPRESS MURDER.

"You don't often read the paper," Madame Baron observed, without looking up. "But I don't suppose our Belgian papers interest you much."

This morning a Brussels bank received by mail from its local branch at Ghent three of the banknotes stolen from M. Van der Cruyssen, who, as our readers will remember, was murdered in the Paris express.

The police were notified at once, and we understand that inquiries are on foot at Ghent to trace the origin of these notes.

In connection with the case our esteemed rival, Le Journal, points out that a curious result will ensue from the difference between French and Belgian law.

It seems that if the crime was committed before the train crossed the border, in Belgian territory, the murderer will be liable only to penal servitude for life, capital punishment being to all intents and purposes obsolete in Belgium.

However, Customs officials are positive that M. Van der Cruyssen, whom they knew by sight, was still alive when the train crossed the border. It follows that the murderer will be tried in France, under French law, and his head may fall under the guillotine.

Conscious of Antoinette's eyes fixed on him, Elie struggled his hardest to assume an air of stoical indifference. But it was more than he could manage. His hands were so clammy that, when he put the paper back on the table, the imprint of his fingers could be seen on it.

Fortunately, just then Baron came downstairs in his railway uniform, and his wife was too busy fussing around him to pay heed to Elie. After filling a Thermos with coffee and milk, she packed some sandwiches in a small tin box he had brought down from his room.

Elie could still see Antoinette's face immediately in front of him, and he was struck by the fixity of the red-flecked pupils. He had a horrid feeling that he was going to faint; an absurd impression that the chair was giving way beneath him. Try as he might, he could not take his eyes off the pale set face confronting him, on which he read a look of growing scorn, scarcely a trace of pity.

"Hope you'll soon get over your cold, Monsieur Elie." The railway man was shaking his hand, but Elie hardly noticed it.

Madame Baron accompanied her husband to the doorstep; a gust of cold air entered the kitchen.

"So you're a coward!" Antoinette exclaimed the moment they were alone.

The words conveyed nothing to Elie. He dimly saw the gleaming tiles of the stove, the yellow mound of potatoes in the enamel pail, the singing kettle, and, in the foreground, the girl's white face. But all these things were so blurred, and seemed to be moving away from him at such a speed, that he brought both hands down heavily on the table to steady himself.

The front door banged, and Madame Baron's footsteps could be heard approaching. Antoinette whispered:

"Be careful."

Her mother eyed each in turn, with a particularly suspicious look for Antoinette. Twice already she had said:

"You might be more polite to Monsieur Elie."

She picked up a potato and her knife.

"If I was you, I'd go out for a bit, cold or no cold. It's half past nine. You sleep much too much, in my opinion."

But he seemed rooted to his chair, incapable of stirring from the kitchen.

"I wouldn't have much use for a man who was always hanging around the house," Antoinette remarked.

"Nobody asked you your opinion, miss! . . . I'm speaking for Monsieur Elie's good, like I was his ma."

He rose with an effort.

"That's better! I've given you a key, haven't I? Now mind you wrap your throat up well."

He lingered for some minutes, sitting on his bed, until the silence of the room, in which every object was already like an old friend, began to work on his nerves. He had only a light overcoat. He put it on, and knotted a woolen muffler around his neck.

Why had Antoinette needed to make him read that article

in the paper? Those horrible last words especially, about his head falling under the guillotine?

Never for a moment had any such idea occurred to him. He forgot to turn off the light. Standing in the hall, he glanced around at the kitchen; through the glazed door he could see Antoinette and her mother still sitting beside the stove, in an atmosphere of quiet so profound that he imagined he heard the ticking of the alarm clock on the mantelpiece.

The moment he stepped outside he started shivering. The sidewalk was like iron underfoot. This was the first time he had seen the street by night, and it looked quite different.

All the houses were in darkness except the grocery, a little to the left. To see other lights he had to look far down the street, where a row of streetlights marked the beginning of the town proper. Nobody was around. The only footsteps audible were a good 500 yards away. Abruptly they stopped, and there was the distant tinkle of a bell, the sound of a closing door.

It was too cold to stand around, and he started walking blindly ahead, his hat pulled down over his eyes, his collar turned up. All the time he had the sensation that he was not in a real street, or on the outskirts of a real town.

The houses were not in an unbroken row, as in most working-class districts, nor were there any side streets. After a block of ten or twelve houses, for instance, all exactly alike, would come an opening, a forlorn field, with sheds and dumps looming up behind it. Then another series of houses, another gap, from which railway tracks shot out across the road. In the background tall chimneys were belching flames into the darkness, and the cold radiance of the sky was mottled with patches of angry red.

Elie had quickened his pace, though quite involuntarily. There was nowhere to go. He passed the windows of a café and saw in it the green rectangle of a billiard table; presumably the one Valesco had referred to.

A family—father, mother, and two children hand in hand

—came down the road toward him, and Elie caught a snatch of their conversation.

"I'm always telling that sister-in-law of yours that she was a crazy fool to . . ."

The last word, or words, escaped him. Suddenly he decided he'd gone far enough. Only 200 yards ahead were lights and shops, and a movie house in which a bell was shrilling. He could see a number of people lined up at the entrance.

Elie stopped and gazed for a moment at the crowd, then turned quickly on his heel. It was all he could do to keep from breaking into a run. He had lost his nerve; he felt as if he were suffocating.

He'd forgotten the key. He walked on, taking long strides, as though escaping from pursuit; indeed, there were moments when he imagined he heard someone at his heels.

At last he saw the Barons' house, the familiar doorway—and he had an impression of having lived there for years and years. The light streaming from the kitchen showed in the keyhole. He didn't ring the bell like a visitor, but rattled the flap of the mail slot.

The eaves were dripping, and big drops splashed down his cheeks. A dark form blotted out the little patch of light and the door opened.

It was Antoinette. Without a word she stood aside to let him enter, her hand resting on the doorknob.

"Brr! It's cold outside!" he muttered.

"You'd better go to bed."

He went into his room and took off his overcoat. He had a vague hope Antoinette would follow him in and, though he made no actual gesture, he fixed his eyes on her imploringly.

"Anything you want?" she asked.

He had an inspiration.

"Well, I'd rather like a fire tonight. It's awfully cold in here."

She made no reply, but she left the door ajar—which

showed she intended to come back. And a moment later he heard a sound that had already become familiar, the sound of coal being shoveled into the scuttle from the heap in the pantry. The two women in the kitchen exchanged some words.

"I'll make a hot toddy for him," said Madame Baron.

Antoinette came back, a scornful look on her face, put down the scuttle, spread a newspaper on the floor, and took off the lid of the stove. It was full of cold cinders, and she had to get down on her knees to empty it.

"Antoinette!" Elie whispered.

She showed no sign of having heard. Sitting on the edge of the bed, his arms dangling, he repeated her name.

"Yes? What do you want?" She spoke in a loud voice.

And suddenly he was afraid. There was a short silence; then he murmured, so softly that he wondered if she heard:

"You're very unkind. . . ."

She made the cinders into a little heap and gathered them on the shovel. Then, crumpling up the newspaper and thrusting it into the stove, she said:

"Have you a match?"

It was such a joy to hear her voice that he rose with clumsy eagerness and started to help her light the fire.

"I don't want your help. I only asked you for a light."

The paper blazed up, and Antoinette dropped a handful of wood upon it. After watching the leaping flames for some moments, suddenly she swung around on Elie.

"Have you got the notes here?"

He hesitated. But her tone had been so imperative that he went to the wardrobe and, standing on tiptoe, brought down the bundle of notes he had hidden on top of it.

"Hand them over!"

Quite naturally, as if she had a perfect right to do so, she dropped the bundle into the flames. Because the fire didn't blaze up at once, she took the poker and stirred the notes to make them catch.

Elie stared at her in silence. He was straining his ears to hear if Madame Baron was still in the kitchen. At last he rose and went up to the girl, holding both his arms out in a gesture of humble entreaty.

"What do you want?" she asked in a matter-of-fact tone, and in her eyes was no anger, no pity; only cool contempt.

"Oh, Antoinette, if you only knew . . ."

"Don't be a fool!" With a laugh she picked up the scuttle and tipped half its contents into the stove. After replacing the lid and making sure with a quick glance that all was in order, she said curtly:

"Now go to bed."

Footsteps receded up the hall, the door of the kitchen shut, and the low murmur of the two women's voices grew fainter.

"Antoinette!" He had called her name aloud without knowing it as he sat dejectedly on the edge of the bed, gazing vaguely in front of him. And suddenly he seemed to see her standing there before him, her body taut under the black dress, the angular shoulders, the young breasts set so oddly far apart, the sides of her small nose flecked with tiny freckles.

Her tone had been cold, not to say hostile, when she told him to go to bed. And yet—! He guessed that he was in her thoughts all day; he knew that, appearances notwithstanding, it was she who listened most attentively when he talked about his home.

"Antoinette!"

He gazed at the empty bed, then at the light switch, and he started sweating again at the mere prospect of the long, dark hours before him. The stove had settled down to a measured roaring, like the noise of an express train. Leaning forward, he had a glimpse of his face in the mirror over the wash basin, and he looked away at once. When taking off his shirt he carefully avoided touching his neck.

His face had the crumpled look of someone's who is weeping, but no tears were in his eyes. When at last he was lying in his bed, in the darkness, he clenched his fists and bit the pillow savagely, muttering to himself: "Antoinette!"

He was afraid, half crazed with fear, and he strained his ears to catch the sounds in the kitchen, where mother and daughter were still at work.

Then he heard Valesco, in the room above, locking his door, and, after some moments, a loud creak of the bed as he stretched himself on it.

7

His watch had stopped, but Elie judged it must be a little after nine, for, looking out his window, he saw the women from the adjoining houses flocking around a vegetable gardener's cart on the far side of the street. It was a frosty morning, and they kept stamping their feet; the nose of one of them, he noticed, a fair-haired young woman, was quite blue with cold. While they were pawing the vegetables in the baskets, the gardener put a tin trumpet to his mouth and blew a long shrill blast—at the first sound of which Madame Baron opened her door and hurried across the street, purse in hand.

There was a knock at Elie's door.

"Come in." He supposed it was Antoinette, coming to replenish the stove.

But it was Valesco who entered. He had a hat and overcoat on, and some books under his arm.

"Well, I must say, you're nice and snug in here. . . . How's the cold today?"

Elie didn't catch on at once, and felt quite pleased by this visit, until the Rumanian, who was gazing out the window, watching Madame Baron haggling for a cauliflower, remarked in a would-be casual tone:

"Say, I wonder if you could do me a small service? Our

worthy landlady's getting in quite a state because my monthly check from home is overdue. That's what she thinks, anyhow. As a matter of fact, it did turn up—ten days ago—but I've blown it all. Could you spare me 300 francs, to tide me over till next week? Got to help each other, haven't we, since we're under the same roof? . . . Oh . . . you use the same kind of razor I do. Strictly between ourselves, though she's very decent in her way, our landlady has old-fashioned ideas about money. Not that she's more grasping than most of that ilk, but—you know what I mean."

Without a word Elie unlocked the suitcase in which he kept his wallet. He had a little over 800 francs, the balance of the note changed at the hairdresser's. He handed three hundred-franc notes to Valesco, who stuffed them into his trouser pocket with rather overdone casualness.

"Do the same for you, old man, another time."

A minute later his head could be seen passing, level with the windowsill, in the direction of town, while in the background the little group of housewives went on ransacking the vegetable gardener's baskets.

Elie had no clear idea of the effect this little incident had produced on him. But somehow it had left him with a load on his mind, which, he had a premonition, would not leave him all day. He stared moodily at the open wallet; then fell to counting what remained. There were five hundred-franc notes, and besides these, he remembered, he had some loose change in his pockets.

Say, 540 francs, all told.

Literally all told—for he had not a cent more in the world. The thousand-franc notes had been burned, except the one he had given to Madame Baron. And that, too, was, to all intents and purposes, as worthless as if it had been destroyed. Antoinette was already aware of this. Quite possibly Madame Baron, too, would get to know it. And a month's board and lodging cost 800 francs!

He hadn't given a thought to this before, and now he was appalled at his predicament. Suppose, for instance, he had to leave at a moment's notice . . .

But no, he wouldn't go away. Really, this was an ideal refuge. "They" would never dream of coming to look for him in a humble, out-of-the-way boardinghouse.

Still, he foresaw trouble ahead. One of these days Madame Baron would be asking him for money, and what would happen then? Right now she made more fuss over him than over the others—simply because he paid the most. He took full board, and was the only one to have meat and vegetables at his evening meal; the only one, too, who had a fire in his room all day. . . .

She had come back to the house. The vegetable seller had moved a little farther up the street. An almost empty streetcar went by. And Elie was still considering, with dismay, the prospect of being turned out of the house for lack of money. It would be nothing short of a disaster! He was sorry now that he had lent those 300 francs to Valesco. But how could he have got out of it? In his present position, wasn't it up to him to make himself agreeable to everybody?

"Monsieur Elie!"

Madame Baron was calling him from the kitchen. When he joined her, he found her taking a frying pan off the stove.

"I'd better give you your breakfast before I go up and do the rooms. How are you feeling today?"

When Baron was out, Elie always used the wickerwork armchair, which gave a shrill, protesting squeak whenever he sat down in it. The kitchen smelled of eggs and bacon. Only Elie's corner of the table was laid.

"Anything else you'd like? I must go upstairs at once, because I've got my ironing this afternoon."

A minute later he heard her talking to Moise, and caught a word or two.

". . . better in the kitchen . . . I've no patience with you . . . overcoat . . . your death of pneumonia!"

And presently Moise came down, carrying some notebooks which, after muttering "Good morning," he dumped on the other end of the table. He started writing at once, in pencil. He had big, gnarled fingers, and pressed so hard on his pencil that the table quivered as he wrote.

Elie hardly knew what he was eating; the thought of the 300 francs he'd given Valesco was rankling in his mind, and, anyway, he had no appetite this morning. He almost envied Moise, who, though he lived on a mere pittance, was sure at least of having enough to pay his board and lodging here.

Moise never looked up. His pudgy hand crawled like a fat, assiduous slug over the paper, his back was hunched, the heat of the fire had brought a glow to his cheeks, and he looked the picture of contentment.

Elie got the coffeepot from the stove and poured himself another cup. Then, after lighting a cigarette, he stared gloomily in front of him, conscious of a curious sense of instability. Acting on a sudden impulse, he addressed Moise in Yiddish:

"Have you been here long?" he asked.

It had struck him that by using Yiddish he would remind the young Jew that there was a bond between them, and make him more favorably disposed.

But, without ceasing to write, Moise replied in French: "A year."

"Don't you speak Yiddish?"

"I speak French, too—and I'm here to improve my French."

At last he had raised his head, and his expression conveyed annoyance at being disturbed at his work. In fact, he looked so hostile that Elie retreated to his bedroom, and fell once more to contemplating the wintry scene in black and white outside: coal-grimed houses, sidewalks sparkling with frost.

The footsteps he could hear in the room immediately above must be Antoinette's, because her mother had gone up to the attic. After listening for a while he went back to the kitchen and picked up a magazine that was lying on the sideboard. Moise had not stirred when he came in, and remained bent over his work.

"Don't you smoke?"

"No."

"Don't you like smoking—or is it to economize?"

No answer. Elie fluttered the pages of the magazine, glancing at the illustrations. He had got in the habit of drinking coffee at all hours, helping himself from the coffeepot, big as an urn, that always stood on the stove. As he poured himself another cup he said to the student:

"Shall I pour you one, too?"

"No, thanks."

"No tobacco. No coffee. And, I wouldn't mind betting, no strong drink either!" He spoke in a bantering tone, with an almost affectionate smile. He was prepared to go to any lengths to break the ice between himself and his taciturn companion. But Moise went on stolidly writing, his furrowed brow propped on his left hand.

How strange to think that for seven years this young man had forgone all the amenities of life in order to carry on his studies! And, Elie could have sworn, had steered clear of women, too!

No, there had been no woman in his life, nor any pleasure but the bleak joy of amassing knowledge. Madame Baron had explained to Elie how Moise would sit poring over his books all day in his fireless room, in a frayed old overcoat, a blanket wrapped around his shoulders; and how at first he used to wash his one and only shirt in the basin, stretching it at arm's length in order to dispense with ironing. Finally, however, she had coaxed him into buying a second shirt, and now she washed his shirt once a week, free of charge.

Three pages were already covered with writing, and apart from the light creak of the pencil and an occasional rattle of the table, there was no sound except the ticking of the alarm clock, which stood at quarter after ten.

"What do you make of me?" Elie asked abruptly. The question had been on the tip of his tongue for several moments, though he hardly knew what prompted him to utter it. All he knew was that he wanted to get on more intimate terms with Moise, who attracted and intimidated him at the same time.

And now at last the Polish Jew looked up and fixed his eyes on Elie; impassive, almost inhuman eyes.

"It's no concern of mine who you may be."

Bitterly offended, Elie got up, and once again—as he did about twenty times a day—walked back to his bedroom. But he found it so boring by himself that very soon he returned to the kitchen.

"Please listen," he said feelingly. "I know that I can trust you, Monsieur Moise, and there's something I'd like you to do—supposing . . . supposing anything happened to me."

Actually, there was no particular service he wanted of the young Jew. But it had occurred to him that by talking in this strain he might jolt the man out of his real, or feigned, indifference. And the words took effect. Moise looked up sharply, and even put down his pencil. Then he said gravely:

"That's enough. Will you kindly drop the subject?"

He rose from his seat. Elie wondered what his next move would be, and he felt the blood rising to his cheeks, his nerves tingling with suppressed excitement. By now he was in the mood to blurt out—almost anything.

"Surely, as members of the same race . . ." he began tentatively.

Moise gathered up his books and papers, and took a step toward the door. In a low tone he said:

"What do you hope to gain by it?"

It wasn't clear if this remark referred to what had just been said, or, in a general way, to Elie's line of conduct.

"Oh, if you take it that way . . ."

"I'm not taking anything in any way. It's none of my business. Still, since you've brought it up, there's one thing I will say. Madame Baron has been most kind to me, and I sincerely hope you won't bring any trouble on her."

He went out without a backward glance, walked slowly through the hall and up the stairs.

Left to himself in the kitchen, Elie felt a rush of hopelessness, a sense of isolation such as he had never known before. The bottom had fallen out of his private universe; there was no foothold anywhere. He had had a similar feeling, though in a milder way, earlier in the morning, when counting the contents of his wallet. . . .

He had brought it on himself, by forcing his advances on Moise. Still, if he had acted thus, wasn't it because he had a feeling that the young man suspected something?

And, though alone, he conjured up an ironically superior smile, to neutralize the snub he had just received, and even murmured to himself: "Of course he's envious of me—that explains it."

He put some more coal on the fire and drew his chair up to it. Noticing that there was hardly any water in the saucepan in which the potatoes were boiling, he got a pitcher and added some. While he was doing this, Madame Baron entered, a pail in each hand. When she saw what he was up to, her face lighted up.

"That's nice of you! You're not like Monsieur Moise, who'll sit there for hours on end with the saucepan right under his nose and never notice nothing, even if the meat's burning to a cinder. Of course he's so wrapped up in his studies he don't notice things like we do. . . ."

Elie accepted the compliment with a modest smile, and sat down again.

"You *must* find it dull here, Monsieur Elie."

"Not in the least, I assure you."

"Still, it's very different from what you're used to, isn't it?

From what you told me, you had such a gay life at home. Really, I can't understand why you don't go out some. When I look at you and Antoinette I sometimes think that she's the boy and you're the girl—if you see what I mean."

He was quite prepared, if she asked him, to do anything: to peel potatoes, even to scour the saucepans. Only one thing mattered: to be allowed to stay here, in this snug little kitchen with the white-enameled walls, whose atmosphere and odors were now more familiar to him than those of his faraway home.

"Antoinette!" Madame Baron shouted. "Don't forget to bring the scuttles down with you."

Elie hadn't seen Antoinette so far that morning, and there was more than curiosity in his eyes when she appeared in the doorway. But she deliberately ignored him, and, carrying the scuttles, walked straight across the room toward the pantry. Her mother scowled at her.

"Well, can't you wish Monsieur Elie 'Good morning'?"

"Good morning."

"Want to be smacked, do you?"

"Oh, please don't scold her!" Elie protested.

"I can't stand manners like that. Especially since you're always so nice and polite to her."

Antoinette gave Elie a long stare with her red-flecked eyes; a stare that seemed to say: "I'll pay you back for that, my man!"

And Elie quailed before her, and shrank back still farther into the armchair, which for some moments had been giving him the queer feeling that it was penning him in, in a wicker-work cage. . . .

The mural decoration of the Merryland was nothing if not modern. The artist had begun by painting a series of wavy blue lines to suggest the sea. Between these were inserted shoals of pink, gold, and vividly green fish, hovering in the same translucent medium as a fishing boat and a larger craft resembling Noah's ark. In the foreground was a broad band of yellow, presumably a beach, on which reclined a bevy of bathing beauties in skillfully seductive poses.

The general effect was colorful, if crude, and, because the room was comparatively small, only a few people were needed to create an atmosphere of gaiety. The lights changed color frequently, which added to the illusion of escape from drab reality.

The night was young, and so far hardly anybody had arrived. The band was playing only for the second set, and the professional dancers were turning up, singly or in pairs, shouting greetings to each other and, as they passed the bar, shaking the bartender's hand. After that they gathered around a corner table, in front of empty champagne glasses, and waited. . . .

In a recess behind a pillar Sylvie was sitting beside the young man with the flowing tie; he had been coming regularly for the last three evenings.

"I can see you're worried about something," he said. "I do wish you'd tell me what it is. Or are you feeling ill?"

She gazed at him with unseeing eyes and answered absentmindedly:

"I'm quite all right, dear."

He squeezed her hand, which he was holding under the table, and said beseechingly:

"Do please confide in me. You know there's nothing in the world I wouldn't do for you."

Smiling, she stroked his hair, which he wore romantically long, but all the time she was watching the door and her thoughts were elsewhere. When Jacqueline appeared, in a moleskin coat, she rose with ill-concealed eagerness, saying to the young man:

"You'll excuse me for a moment, won't you? I have something to say to the girl who's just come in."

The cloakroom attendant helped Jacqueline out of her coat; after which Sylvie led her to the bar.

"Well?"

"So far all's gone well. But, as I was coming in, I thought I saw a fellow snooping around the entrance. I asked Joseph if he'd noticed him, and he said 'Yes'; the man had been standing there for an hour or so."

The cabaret was still almost empty. The manager, in evening clothes, was at his usual place at the head of the stairs, gazing lethargically into the room.

"I see your young man's here again," Jacqueline remarked. "Poor kid—it's quite pathetic!"

"Yesterday I told him to stop coming, and what do you think? He burst into tears! . . . Do you know, the cigarette girl stuck him for twenty-five francs for a pack of cigarettes just now! I told her it was a dirty trick; he can't afford it."

But the thoughts of both were far from the young poet's troubles. It was Jacqueline who spoke first.

"Well, what has to be done next?"

"I wish I knew. . . . Bob, mix me one with a kick in it."

She drank at a gulp the cocktail the barman handed her; then knit her brows, thinking hard. Her eyes were fixed on the young poet sitting on the banquette, but she saw him dimly, like a figure seen through badly focused glasses. At last she said:

"Now that they've traced the notes to Ghent . . ." Then she fell silent again.

"Look," Jacqueline said, "I propose we eat, to start with. I can't face trouble on an empty stomach, and, by the look of things, they'll be around here soon."

Just then a telephone purred. When the manager went off to answer it, Sylvie cocked an ear in his direction, for she had a feeling that the call concerned her.

"Wait here," she said.

As she stepped out to the landing, the manager was returning from the telephone booth.

"Oh, good! There you are! The call's for you."

"Hello?" She spoke in a low tone, so as not to be overheard by the manager, who was only a few yards away.

"Is that Mademoiselle Sylvie?" a voice asked. "I want to talk to Mademoiselle Sylvie herself."

"Yes, it's me."

"It's the porter at the Palace speaking." He dropped his voice till it was barely audible. "Listen! The police have just been here. They've found out about your having stayed here with Monsieur Nagear. I thought I'd better let you know, in case . . ."

The manager had his eyes on her as she walked back to the bar. She gave a smile in passing to her young poet, who gazed at her adoringly.

"We're in for it!" she told Jacqueline.

"What do you mean?"

"They've found out about the Palace. Where are the notes?"

"In my bag."

"Hand it over."

Under cover of the projecting edge of the big mahogany bar Sylvie managed to extract the notes without being seen, and slipped them under her bodice.

"What do you plan to do? And how about *me*? What should I say?"

"Oh, you're safe enough. I only asked you to change the notes. You knew nothing about them."

"And that's the truth. When I went to Ghent I didn't know . . ."

Two couples were dancing. Furtively Sylvie squeezed her friend's fingers.

"Don't worry, pet. Leave it to me."

When he saw her coming back to him, the young man beamed with delight.

"Your friend's nowhere near as pretty as you are," he exclaimed with naïve eagerness. "What'll you drink?"

"We've had a drink already."

"Yes, but he's taken the glasses away."

She scowled at the waiter, though, after all, he was only doing his duty in obliging customers to order drinks.

"All right. An orangeade."

In some way it was a nuisance having this sentimental youth on her hands; still, his company made the situation easier than if she'd been alone. Though Jacqueline had turned up, Sylvie continued watching the door, and once again she had a presentiment—on hearing heavy footsteps coming up the stairs, and the voice of the manager, announcing:

"This way, sir. The show's just going to start."

But no one entered, nor was there any sound but that of the clubroom door opening and closing. Officially, the Merryland passed for a private club; this enabled alcoholic drinks to be served on the premises. And, for appearance' sake, a small room on the other side of the landing had been fixed up as a reading room, with magazines strewn on the table, and two big leather armchairs.

"Does this . . . this gay life really give you pleasure?" The young man blushed at his audacity.

Without stopping to think, she answered almost angrily:

" 'Gay' do you call it?"

But she let it go at that. What was the point of trying to explain things to this guileless youth? She was cocking her ear toward the clubroom, though she knew it was quite impossible to hear what was being said there.

Jacqueline, who was wearing her mauve silk dress, had chosen a seat beside the band, and had already danced twice. The young man said timidly:

"I hope you're not offended. I shouldn't have asked you that."

"Offended? Not a bit."

Her one desire was for him to keep his mouth shut, since her nerves were stretched. At any moment the manager's portly form would show up in the doorway. At last she could bear the suspense no longer.

"Excuse me for a moment."

She jumped up and hurried to the bar.

"Give me another cocktail. Quick!"

No sooner had she drunk it than she saw the manager at the door, beckoning to her.

She stole a quick glance at her reflection, sandwiched between two bottles, in the mirror behind the bar, patted her hair, and whispered to the bartender:

"Tell Jacqueline there's nothing to worry about."

The manager watched her coming toward him.

"There's a man here . . ." he began.

"I know."

She opened the door of the clubroom, and as she closed it she saw a man of about forty in an overcoat with a velvet collar, pretending to be looking at the pictures in a magazine.

"You're Sylvie Baron, eh? Sit down, please."

He showed her a card with "Detective Inspector" under his name.

"Know why I've come, Mademoiselle Baron?"

"Of course."

She saw that he was taken aback by her prompt "Of course."

"Good. I'm glad to hear you say that. It'll make things easier. I need hardly tell you that I will be questioning your friend Jacqueline presently—and that I know a good deal more than you suspect."

"Really?"

The room was as bare as the parents' waiting room in a small school, or a clinic. Indeed, the only difference was that the air was throbbing with the muffled stridence of a jazz band.

"Now then," the detective said, "let's hear what you have to say."

"I'll answer your questions."

He looked reassuringly human and had already bestowed appreciative glances on the low vee of Sylvie's dress.

"Are you acquainted with a man named Elie or Elias Nagear?"

"You know I am. You only had to look at the register at the Palace."

"Where did you first meet him?"

"On board the *Théophile-Gautier*. He got on at Constantinople."

"And you became his mistress?"

"His mistress? That's much too big a word for it. We happened to be traveling together all the way to Brussels, and naturally we got a little friendly."

"Do you mean to say you weren't his mistress?"

She shrugged her shoulders, and sighed.

"That's not the word for it, as I said just now. If you can't see the difference . . ."

"Did you know that Nagear was short of money?"

"He never talked to me about money."

"Did he ever tell you, or imply, that he was going to commit a crime?"

She looked him in the eyes.

"Look here! What's the good of beating about the bush? I wasn't born yesterday, and of course I can see what you're driving at. If he's committed a crime, I know nothing about it. All I know is that when I left the hotel room last Wednesday at about eleven he was still in bed with a bad cold. I had lunch out, and when I came back late in the afternoon I found him gone."

"What about his luggage?"

She thought quickly. Almost certainly he had learned at the Palace that she'd gone out next day with Elie's luggage.

"Oh, he left it at the hotel."

"Quite so. And when did Nagear return?"

She stood up—it was easier to think standing—and the detective followed her with his eyes as she paced up and down the room.

"He called me up from the station and asked me to bring his luggage, because he had a train to catch."

"Yes? What did you do then?"

The detective had slipped the rubber band off a small notebook, in which he scribbled away.

"I did what he asked. He gave me 50,000 francs, and then took the Warsaw express."

He looked up at her sharply, but she didn't turn a hair.

"Oh, he took the Warsaw train, did he? What time was that?"

She smiled to herself—for she had down pat the times of all the international expresses. She'd taken them often enough for that!

"Nine-thirty-six. Nagear apologized for leaving me so abruptly and, as I said, gave me 50,000 francs."

She put her hand down her dress, produced the little wad of notes, and laid them on the table.

"In Belgian notes?" The detective sounded surprised.

"No, in French notes."

"Ah, you changed them! In Brussels, I suppose."

"You know quite well I didn't. And you know, too, that girls like us are always suspected of having done something wrong when they're seen with a lot of money on them. I got a friend of mine to change the notes in Ghent and Antwerp."

"Did you have no suspicion? Didn't you check the numbers?"

"I never read the newspapers."

"Then how is it you know now?"

"Bob, the bartender here, told me what had happened to

Van der B—" She pulled herself up. "Van der Cruyssen, and I guessed. . . ."

"Then why didn't you assist justice by making a report to the police?"

"Assist justice? Why should I? That's your job, not mine."

There was something like a smile on her face; indeed, her self-possession was amazing. And while she spoke she never took her eyes off the detective.

"That's all very well, but suppose I hadn't got on your trail?"

"I knew you would, sooner or later."

"Are you prepared to confirm on oath the statements you have just made?"

"Certainly . . . And now, if you have nothing more to ask, I'd like to go back to the dancing. Any objection?"

She gave him a quick smile, and he, too, was smiling as he snapped the rubber band around his notebook.

"*Au revoir,*" she said, her fingers on the door handle.

"Yes. I'll see you again later."

The manager had hardly time to step away from the keyhole, but Sylvie walked past him as if she hadn't noticed anything. Jacqueline was drinking champagne with two men in dinner jackets, an elderly man and a young one, father and son perhaps. With a flutter of her eyelashes Sylvie conveyed to her that all was going smoothly.

The young poet was moping in a corner; he seemed to have given up hope of seeing her again that evening, for he looked quite startled when he saw her coming.

"Hope you haven't been too bored," she said.

"No . . . not at all. I was waiting for you." The mere sight of her had made him blush, and to cover his confusion he asked: "Won't you have something to drink?"

"What? Has that damn waiter taken away the glasses again? Really, he's the limit." Seeing him go by, she shouted at him: "Henri, didn't I tell you . . . ?"

"It doesn't matter in the least," the young man broke in.

She looked him full in the eyes, and he started blushing again. Even his ears went scarlet. Suddenly she asked:

"Are you living with your parents?"

"No. They're in Liège. I have a little room, a sort of attic really, in the Schaerbeek district. But when my book comes out . . ."

The manager had left his post at the top of the stairs and gone down to the dancing room in order to have a better view of Sylvie. Jacqueline was giggling as she nibbled the green almonds she had persuaded the man beside her to order, and constantly throwing questioning glances at Sylvie over her shoulder.

"Do you really like being here?" Sylvie asked.

"Well—er—not really. But so long as I'm with you . . ."

Bob, too, was staring at her; as, indeed, were all the staff. Obviously the word had gone around.

"Pay."

"Do you want me to go?"

"We'll go to your place."

"But—!" He was horrified at the idea of taking an elegant young woman like Sylvie to his attic.

"Do what I tell you, my dear. It isn't Sunday every day of the week."

As he counted his change he looked profoundly puzzled. It wasn't Sunday—so what on earth did she mean by that last remark?

"No, we don't need a taxi," she said to the doorman as they stepped to the sidewalk. And, linking her arm with the young man's, she said, almost affectionately: "Let's take a streetcar."

8

Now and again Elie opened his eyes and saw heads bobbing past, level with his windowsill, in the bleak morning light. He learned it was Friday, for among the others he saw Madame Baron go by with a hat on—which meant that she was on her way to the weekly market in the square. Domb, too, had gone out, and a sound of slippered footsteps overhead told him that Valesco was up and dressing.

For the fourth or fifth time he dozed off; he made a point of staying in bed until the other lodgers had gone out and he could be sure of having the place to himself. The trouble was that every five minutes the clanging of a streetcar jerked him awake and, since the stop was almost in front of his window, it was hopeless trying to get to sleep till it had started off again.

The postman passed. A letter rattled through the mail slot, and Elie was of half a mind to get up and see whom it was for; but his energy failed him and he rolled over, with his face toward the wall. How much more time went by? In a half-dream he seemed to hear Valesco go out. Then, with the dramatic suddenness of a shot fired in a crowd, his door banged. Someone had come in, and before Elie had time to turn his head, a hand snatched back the spread, which he had pulled up over his chin.

Something, perhaps the rustle of a dress, perhaps a whiff of scent, told him it was Antoinette; otherwise he'd have postponed opening his eyes. Her face was so white that the freckles showed like angry blotches. With a severe look she handed him a sheet of paper.

"Read this."

"What time is it?"

"Damn the time! Read it!"

For some moments he played the part of a man only half awake, while she stood, silent and hostile, at the bedside. At last, screwing up his eyes, he read:

Antoinette, use your brains and try to understand. . . . The new lodger has got to leave at once. It's terribly important. You may have trouble, since he seems to have dug himself in, but he's got to go. Tell him from me that the police know everything and his name will be in the papers within the next few hours. He still has time to make a getaway. Don't tell Ma. Your affectionate sister, Sylvie.

Though he had read the letter a dozen times, Elie seemed unable to take his eyes off it. And Antoinette, who in her black pinafore looked like a schoolgirl waiting her turn to say her lesson, finally lost her patience.

"Well? What about it?"

He was sitting on the edge of the bed, barefooted; his pajama jacket was unbuttoned and revealed a lean, rather hairy chest. Slowly his fingers parted, letting the letter drop on the rug, but then they clenched and unclenched, as if kneading some invisible object. Antoinette's face hardened.

"Stop being a fool!"

Immediately the hands stopped moving. Elie raised his head, but so far he hadn't settled on an expression, or decided what line to take. His forehead was deeply furrowed; whether with distress or thought it was impossible to tell. But there was a wary look in his eyes, a glint of anger and suspicion.

"Do you really want to turn me out?" he murmured brokenly, striking a pose of profound dejection.

"Whether I want it or not, you've got to go."

The letter itself hadn't been much of a surprise. It was Antoinette's remark that made him lose all self-control. From then on he was no longer playacting, and there was something so shocking in this sudden breakdown of his morale that the girl was, for the first time, really scared.

He rose slowly to his feet, and the movement brought his face within a few inches of hers. His lips were twitching, there was frenzy in his eyes, his breath came in feverish gasps.

"So you'd betray me to my enemies, would you?"

She wanted to look away, but a horrid fascination, like that which draws a crowd to watch the struggles of a man who has just been run over, held her eyes on him.

"Answer me!"

His face was gray, unwashed, unshaven, and sweat was pouring down it. His pajamas were soiled and crumpled. The sight of his abject fear made her feel sick.

"Don't!" She shrank away.

"Antoinette! Look into my eyes."

She could feel his hot breath fanning her cheeks, and it was all she could do to keep from screaming.

"Look at me! I insist. Don't forget I have a sister, too. Suppose you had a brother and . . . and he was in my position."

Suddenly, to her consternation, he fell on his knees before her, clasped her hands in his.

"Don't say such cruel things. Please, please don't tell me to go. Once I leave this house I'm finished, and you know it. It will be all your fault. I . . . I don't want to die."

"Get up."

"Not before you've promised . . ."

She drew back two steps, but he shuffled after her, on his knees.

"Antoinette! Promise me you won't do that. You remember what they said in the paper, don't you? In France . . ."

"Oh, for heaven's sake shut up!" she almost screamed.

As she spoke her body suddenly grew rigid, her heart gave a lurch. A head had just passed the window, stopping a moment on the way. It was Madame Baron, returning from her marketing, and unthinkingly she had glanced into the room.

A key grated in the door; she heard it open. Then came a soft thud as Madame Baron deposited her shopping bag on the hall floor.

"Get up!"

It was too late. Already Madame Baron's plump black-clad form was looming in the doorway. She had a hat on, and this made her look more stern and dignified than usual. She gazed first at her daughter, then at the man in pajamas rising awkwardly to his feet.

"Go up to your room," she said to Antoinette, after a moment's hesitation. "And look sharp about it. I'll talk to you later."

She was holding herself in. No sooner was her daughter out of the room than she shut the door with a bang and rounded on Elie.

"Well, you dirty swine, ain't you ashamed of yourself—making up to a little girl half your age? What you deserve is a good hiding, and I've a very good mind . . ."

She actually raised her fist, and he shrank away, shielding his head with his arm.

But then her eyes fell on his face and she noticed that his cheeks were deathly pale, glistening with tears and sweat. And suddenly, to her amazement, he started trembling violently, breathing with a sort of rattle, his teeth chattering convulsively.

Mistrustfully she watched him back into a corner of the room and start pounding the wall with his clenched fists.

"What on earth's come over you?"

The harsh, vulgar voice was like a summons back to reality,

but it had no effect on Elie. He went on beating the wall, and she seemed to hear him whimper:

"Mother! Oh, Mother . . . !"

All his manhood had left him. In the loosely fitting pajamas he looked like an emaciated, half-starved child in the grip of panic terror.

"Going crazy, are you?"

As she spoke she noticed the letter lying on the floor, and recognized Sylvie's writing.

She read the letter, though there was no need to do so; suddenly the truth—of which till now she had not had the faintest inkling—had dawned on her. As she looked up from the letter, Elie swung around and faced her, still trembling with emotion, his hands pressed to the wall behind him as if bracing himself to spring forward.

"So that's it," Madame Baron said, letting the letter slip from her fingers. Then her legs seemed to give way and she leaned heavily on the table. "Well, I never! What a fool I've been! I never suspected a thing. Of course, I must say, you went about it cleverly."

She had a feeling that he was going to clasp her hands, perhaps go down on his knees to her as well, and start imploring her. . . . Gruffly she said:

"None of that nonsense! It won't work with me. Get dressed and clear out—at once! Got it? If I find you here in a quarter of an hour's time, I'll have the police in."

She began to move toward the door, but stopped abruptly, halted by the most appalling sound that had ever reached her ears—one of those long-drawn-out screams that are only heard in moments of supreme catastrophe, when voices lose all semblance of humanity and sound like the squeals of dying animals.

Elie had staggered to the bed and flung himself across it, his arms spread out, his fingers scrabbling on the spread, and he went on screaming, arching his body like someone in convulsions. Now and again, between screams, came that low, desperate, whimpered "Mother!"

Madame Baron glanced nervously toward the window, afraid passers-by would hear; then back again at the writhing form on the bed.

"Calm down!" she said, and was surprised by the sound of her voice. "If you go on making that noise, we'll have all the neighbors in." She took a step toward him, and added in a less assured tone: "You know, you can't possibly stay on in this house."

She took off her hat wearily and dropped it on the table.

"Now do try to pull yourself together. You've still got time to get away without being caught."

She walked hastily to the door, and listened; then turned the key and came back to the bed.

"Please pay attention, Monsieur Elie. I'm speaking for your own good. . . ."

The kitchen was empty, the alarm clock ticking away for its own benefit alone, the kettle singing to itself, filling the air with steam. Now and then a shower of red cinders would rattle through the grate into the pan below. The windowpanes were misted over.

Only one end of the table was laid—at Elie's place—and his breakfast, two eggs and a slice of bacon, stood waiting to be cooked, on a plate at the side of the stove.

The shopping bag, from which the heads of a bundle of leeks protruded, remained where Madame Baron had left it, beside the front door.

The only sounds in the room were the ticking of the clock and an occasional tinkle of the kettle lid. Never had the house seemed so forsaken. Every door was shut, and for once no pails of water, no mops or brooms were lying about in the hall. There was an atmosphere of hushed suspense, like that when some great domestic event is impending—when, for instance, everyone is waiting for a woman to have a baby.

Presently a sound of footsteps came from Elie's bedroom. The door emitted a loud creak, as though it were being opened for the first time in years. Carrying her hat, Madame Baron walked past her shopping bag, unheeding; then remembered, and went back to get it.

On entering the kitchen she was half suffocated by the cloud of steam that greeted her, and, hurrying to the window, she opened it a few inches, letting in a gush of icy air.

There was a whole series of ritual gestures to be performed, and she went through them methodically, with an unusually thoughtful look on her face. She took the almost empty kettle off the stove and filled it at the faucet; she placed a saucepan on the fire, then hung her hat on a peg and unpacked the vegetables on the portion of the table that was not set. Finally she glanced at the clock. It showed twenty past ten.

Taking a paring knife from the drawer and putting on an apron, she walked back to the hall, and shouted:

"Monsieur Moise!"

Only then did her feelings get the better of her; the second time she called, her voice broke on a sob. And, on returning to the kitchen, she wiped her eyes and nose with a corner of her apron.

There were footsteps overhead, and presently Moise came down the stairs. Madame Baron was skinning onions for the stew, but the onions did not account for the tears in her eyes. Moise noticed them at once, and, frowning heavily, inquired:

"What's wrong, Madame Baron?"

"Please sit down, Monsieur Moise. I have something to tell you." She avoided looking at him, but he could still see her face, and it was so woebegone that he lowered his eyes. "I know I can trust you, Monsieur Moise. It's something I don't even dare tell my husband. You know how he is; he'd only start bawling the roof off, and that wouldn't take us any further, would it?" She blew her nose and, bending forward, slowly closed the door of the stove. "I don't know how to start. . . . First of all, though, you must promise not to breathe a word of this to anyone."

She was cutting up the onions and letting the slices fall into the blue enamel saucepan.

"I've just learned that our new lodger, Monsieur Elie . . ."

She happened to look up, and the first glance was enough.

"What! You knew it? . . . And I was so silly I never suspected a thing! I treated him just like the other lodgers; in fact, I made a fuss over him. What a fool I was! This morning I told him he had to go. I didn't like doing it, but seeing as my husband's a government employee . . ." She paused abruptly, her knife suspended in mid-air; a hateful picture of the scene in Elie's bedroom had risen before her eyes. "I never dreamed a man could get in such a state. In all my born days I've never seen nothing like it, not even in the movies. He bit his lips till the blood came, and he kept howling for his ma."

Unconsciously she was glancing over her shoulder toward the hall and the door behind which that dreadful scene had taken place.

"You know what they do to . . . to murderers in France, don't you?" And when he made no answer, she added, with a nervous sob: "They chop their heads off!"

Dropping the onion and knife on the table, she lifted her apron with both hands and hid her face in it. Moise murmured awkwardly:

"Oh, Madame Baron . . . please don't take on like that!"

Her shoulders heaved and, her face still hidden in the apron, she said weakly:

"Don't take no notice. I'll be better in a minute. Only, it was such a shock, you know. . . ."

Timidly Moise laid his hand on her shoulder; that was as far as he dared go.

"If you'd seen him!" she moaned. "He looked like such a poor miserable little shrimp, shivering and shaking in his pajamas, like a kid that's scared out of his wits. One couldn't help but be sorry for him. All skin and bone . . ."

"Madame Baron, do please compose yourself. You'll only make yourself ill."

She wiped her eyes and cheeks and, as she smoothed out her apron, conjured up a feeble smile.

"There! I'm better now."

The window had blown open. She went and closed it.

"I may have made a mistake. But he swore to me that if I let him stay a few days longer, he'd be safe. He has 500 francs left; I saw them. But 500 won't take him far."

A new thought waylaid her. She raised the lid of the soup tureen and, after fumbling feverishly in it, dropped the thousand-franc note into the fire.

"I'd never have breathed a word of this to anyone else. But I know you'll give me good advice, Monsieur Moise. Don't you agree that we can let him stay on for a day or two more? The police think he's miles away, and anyhow they'd never dream of looking for him in a quiet little house like this, would they?" Afraid she had not yet convinced him, she added: "It was when he spoke about his ma. . . . Somehow it made me think of yours, Monsieur Moise. Of course, if all he had to be afraid of was being sent to prison, it would be quite different. You see what I mean, don't you?"

She had started peeling onions again, and her eyes were watery, though not now with tears. She was still snuffling a little, but her composure was returning.

"Good gracious! I'll never have lunch ready in time at this rate. . . . We have Monsieur Domb and Monsieur Valesco to think of, don't forget. If there's anything about him in the papers, they're bound to notice. If that happens, I'd rather it was you who told them."

Her thoughts took a new turn.

"Have you seen Antoinette around?"

"I heard her going to her bedroom a while ago."

She opened the door and shouted: "Antoinette!"

No answer. No sound of an opening door overhead. Still carrying her paring knife, Madame Baron hurried up the stairs.

"What are you doing up there?"

Antoinette was doing nothing. There was no heating of any kind in her room, and though the skylight was shut tight, cold air was seeping in, owing, perhaps, to the thinness of the glass.

Antoinette was lying on her bed, gazing up at the slanted ceiling.

"Why didn't you answer when I called?"

Never before had Madame Baron seen that strange, set look in her daughter's eyes, or her face so deathly calm. Indeed, there was something so disquieting about it that she hurried to the bed and gave her arm a little tug.

"Well? What do you want?" the girl said fretfully.

"You gave me quite a turn! Come downstairs. You'll catch your death of cold if you stay up here. . . . Why are you looking at me like that?"

· "Where is he?"

"In his room." How was she to explain things to her daughter? "You wouldn't understand," she said vaguely, "but I have my reasons. I've told him he can stay a few days longer. But you're not to have anything to do with him. If he speaks to you, don't answer."

Antoinette seemed to wake up with a start, giving her head a curious backward jerk, as if her neck had gone numb and she had to free it."

"What I can't get over," her mother said, "is the silliness of Sylvie—to let herself be mixed up in that sort of thing. . . . Come along."

They went downstairs together. When Moise saw Antoinette he was startled by her changed appearance.

"I'll talk to Domb and Valesco," he said hastily.

"Thanks . . . Antoinette, go and get the butter from the pantry." She bestowed a smile of gratitude on Moise. "That's very kind of you, I'm sure. . . . I'm doing the right thing, don't you agree?"

By way of answer Moise, too, smiled vaguely; then he started toward the stairs.

"Why not come and study by the fire?" she called after him.

Apparently he didn't hear.

The life of the house resumed its usual course. The onions began to sizzle on the stove, while Madame Baron started to chop up the meat for the stew. Suddenly, without looking up from her work, she said to her daughter:

"You know what your dad's like; it wouldn't do for him to know. You'd better look through the paper before he reads it and, if there's anything, tear the page off."

Antoinette, too, made no reply.

"Now go and do up Monsieur Domb's room. Don't forget it's the day to change the sheets."

At half past eleven Baron appeared. He had been on duty all night and had the rest of the day off. After hanging his coat on a peg in the hall, he entered the kitchen, sniffed the air, and asked:

"Grub ready?"

"In a few minutes."

His wife placed his slippers in front of the wicker armchair, and Baron proceeded to take off his boots, socks, and collar.

"Terrible cold it can be round about Luxembourg. This morning just after sunrise we saw a boar floundering around in the snow."

"Is there much snow there?"

"Nearly four foot deep in places."

She was taking care to keep her back toward him, but a moment came when he had a glimpse of her face.

"What's wrong with you?"

"Wrong with me?"

"Your eyes are all red."

"Oh, that's the onions." She pointed to the onion skins on the table.

"Hurry up with my grub. I want to get to bed."

She bustled about, took the potatoes from the oven, where they had been browning, and set the table. Valesco entered, bringing wafts of frozen air lodged in the folds of his overcoat.

"Sorry, Monsieur Valesco, but I must ask you to wait a bit. My husband's been on duty all night and I'll give him his lunch first."

"Has my friend been around this morning?"

"No one's been. Oh, by the way, you'd better go up to Monsieur Moise's room. He has something to tell you."

"Something to tell me? What on earth can it be?"

She didn't feel at ease till she heard his footsteps on the stairs.

"Has he paid?" asked Monsieur Baron.

"Yes, he settled up yesterday. What's more, he brought a cake for supper; I've kept a slice for you."

"Where's Antoinette?"

"Doing the rooms. She was a little late this morning getting started."

He began eating by himself, sometimes pausing to push up his straggling gray mustache.

"No news from Sylvie?"

"Our Sylvie never was one for letter-writing—you should know that."

To conceal her nervousness Madame Baron busied herself with her pots and pans. When Domb entered, after bowing to her from the doorway, Baron was drinking his coffee and finishing the slice of cake.

"Lunch ready, Madame Baron?"

"In a couple of minutes, Monsieur Domb."

He always gave the impression of extreme cleanliness, as if, unlike the other lodgers, he never omitted a morning bath. With another bow he started to leave the kitchen.

"Where are you off to?"

"I thought of going to my room."

"Why not wait here? You're not in the way at all." Madame Baron was always a little flustered by the Pole's exaggerated courtesy. "There's a chair. The others will be here in a moment."

Baron rose, yawned, stretched his arms, and said to his wife:

"Don't forget to wake me at four."

On his way out he planted a clumsy kiss on his wife's hair, while she called toward the doorway:

"Monsieur Valesco! Monsieur Moise! Antoinette! Lunch!"

To divert attention from her reddened eyes, she tried to put on a more smiling face than usual. It was only when she heard the footsteps of the young folk on the stairs that it struck her she'd forgotten someone.

"Monsieur Elie! Come to lunch."

Some tense moments followed, while the others took their seats around the table. At last Madame Baron, who was listening intently, heard a key turn in a lock and the creak of an opening door.

While she was putting coal on the fire and stirring it with the poker, she heard the kitchen door open and shut and "Good mornings" being exchanged.

At last she turned, and saw Elie at his usual place, his cheeks only a shade paler than usual, only a hint of discomposure in his eyes. He had shaved, his hair was smoothly brushed, and, as he took the plate that was handed him, he said to Antoinette in a low but steady voice:

"May I trouble you for the bread, Mademoiselle?"

Was it because today he was wearing a collar and a tie? For some reason Antoinette's gaze settled on his neck. Then, with startling suddenness, she jumped up from her chair and, before anyone could say a word, ran out, slamming the door behind her.

Madame Baron started to follow, but thought better of it.

"She's not feeling very well today," she explained.

Moise, who didn't get the same meal as the others—it cost five francs—extracted from his tin box a loaf and a pat of butter, and put them on the table. Like an orchestra tuning up, there began a confused, steadily increasing noise, the rattle of knives and forks on plates, a chink of glasses, and when at last a voice made itself heard above these sounds, it was Elie's.

"It's terribly cold outdoors, isn't it?"

It was his ordinary voice, a trifle thickened perhaps by the food he had in his mouth.

No one answered.

9

The water pitcher in Moise's attic room had burst, and for several days thereafter the block of ice that had done the mischief could be seen glimmering, like a translucent cannonball, in a corner of the yard.

At all times voices, plaintive or indignant, could be heard protesting:

"The door's open again! For heaven's sake shut it!"

The temperature was far below freezing point, but the sky was cloudless, the air crystal-clear; indeed, there were four consecutive days of brilliant sunshine.

"Do please shut the door!" wailed Madame Baron.

The kitchen was the only warm place in the house, and everyone made use of it from early morning on. The lodgers went there, one after the other, to get hot water, and, since it was impossible to heat enough water for all at once, hung around the stove in their pajamas, waiting their turn. The first thing Madame Baron did each day was to strew salt on the doorstep and the sidewalk in front, where ice had formed overnight, and when she came back to the kitchen her fingers were numb with cold, her nose was scarlet.

There was always a scuffle for the place nearest the fire,

though as a matter of fact the cold seemed more productive of good-humor than otherwise. Even the children running past the house on their way to school, their faces wrapped in balaclavas, were hoping that the frost would last, the mercury fall still lower. The next-door neighbor, whose pipes had burst, kept dropping in at all hours for water, a pail in each hand.

"It seems the Zuider Zee is beginning to freeze over."

Everyone was thrilled—Elie no less than the others. He was the first each morning to go out to read the thermometer they had hung up in the yard. On his return to the kitchen he would announce the latest figure with an air of triumph.

"Twenty degrees, Fahrenheit! But of course we register far lower temperatures than that in Anatolia, almost every winter."

His eyes roved around the table from one face to another. Domb never responded, but Elie made a point of feigning not to notice this. Valesco now and then gave a polite smile, to show that he was listening. Moise, in any case, never took part in conversations.

"One year I started off from Trebizond in my car to go to Iran, where my father had business interests. . . . I suppose you know that practically all the traffic in those parts consists of camel caravans."

"What? Ain't there no railway?" Baron seemed surprised.

"Not yet. The plans have been drawn up, but that's as far as they have got. Only imagine the distances to cover! We count them in thousands of miles in our part of Europe."

Actually Baron was now the only one to display much interest in Elie's chatter. He may have been a trifle puzzled by the reserved attitude of the others, but it wasn't marked enough for him to comment on it.

Elie, on the other hand, was more loquacious than ever. He had got over his cold and stiff neck, ate heartily, and went on having, unlike the other lodgers, a full dinner every night. Indeed, he had never seemed in better shape.

On the first night everybody had eyed him curiously as he

piled his plate with meat and vegetables, while the others were content with bread and butter. But he seemed quite unconscious of their scrutiny. Noticing a plate of cheese in front of Baron, he asked politely:

"That Roquefort looks excellent. Would you mind passing it?"

Antoinette, however, seemed to have lost her appetite completely, and her father was quite worried.

"You're not looking at all well, dear. I've never seen your face so peaked. I suppose it's something to do with your age. Growing pains, most likely. But that's all the more reason to eat well."

Elie promptly put in a remark.

"Yes, my sister got like that when she was Antoinette's age. In fact, we were afraid of losing her, and Mother sent her off to Greece for a change of air. Ever been in Greece?"

"It's just thoughtlessness," Madame Baron whispered to Moise. "He don't seem to realize . . ."

Earlier in the day he had told her in a quite matter-of-fact tone:

"You know, you needn't worry, Madame Baron, about the money I owe you. I've written to my sister, and it should be here in a week's time."

She had thought it wiser not to reply, and busied herself with her cooking. But when she noticed him picking up the bag of mussels she had bought that morning, and opening a drawer to get a knife, she couldn't help remarking:

"Whatever are you up to?"

"Oh, I'm going to give you a hand at trimming these mussels."

"Please don't bother, Monsieur Elie."

"It's not the least bother. I like doing it."

He was constantly in the kitchen. Sometimes she managed to get him out of it, but he nearly always came back in a few minutes, on some pretext or other.

"Look, I've got to wash the floor," she would say. "Please go to your room."

He thought up another trick; he left his bedroom door ajar, and no one could enter or leave the house without being hailed by him.

"Hello, Valesco! Come and warm your hands for a minute. Madame Baron wants the kitchen to herself just now. A cigarette? . . . You see how right I was! There's not a word about me in the papers today."

He was always the first to read them, and would even snatch Baron's *Gazette* from his hand when he was settling down to read it.

"May I have just a peep? . . . Thanks so much."

When satisfied that there was no reference to himself, he handed the paper back, with a wink to the others around the table and a murmured "All's well!"

In a flutter of anxiety, Madame Baron watched her husband's face, but he never seemed to notice anything odd in Elie's conduct.

All of them did their best to avoid being buttonholed by Elie on their way through the hall, or at the kitchen door—but there was no escaping him. Time and again Madame Baron begged him to stay in his room and keep the door shut.

"But I'd so much rather be with you!" he would reply.

And she never could summon up the courage to tell him frankly that his presence made her feel uncomfortable.

It had the same effect on everyone in the house, with the exception of Baron, who still had no suspicion of any kind. The others, when they wanted to discuss the situation, were reduced to taking refuge in the attic or on the first-floor landing. Even so, Elie, who had sharp ears, would say the moment they came down:

"Been talking about me, haven't you?"

"Don't be silly! Do you imagine we have nothing else to talk about?"

"I'm sure that was it. But you have no reason to feel worried. In a few days' time they'll have forgotten all about me, and I will make a move. And, of course, once I'm back home, I'll send you all nice remembrances."

He seemed to have completely forgotten that humiliating scene in the bedroom, his abasement, his tears. It was as if he'd never gone down on his knees to Antoinette, never sobbed and whimpered for his mother, never implored Madame Baron to forgive him, his face so livid that she thought he was going to have a fit. Never could she forget the way he had beaten his hands against the wall, or how he'd sprawled on the bed, jerking his limbs like an epileptic.

Somehow or other he had blotted all that out of his memory, had resumed his place in the household as if nothing had happened. True, his board and lodging were unpaid, since the banknote was burned; but he was lavish with promises of the presents he would send once he was back in Turkey.

"Before I leave I'll show you how to make Turkish coffee, and once I'm back I'll send you a real Turkish coffee set of burnished copper."

There were moments when Madame Baron felt like going on her knees to him and begging him to keep quiet. She could not even have a minute's quiet talk with her daughter. No sooner had they settled down together in the kitchen than the door opened, and there he was! In fact, he seemed to regard the kitchen as his domain, and fifty times a day walked the length of the hall between his bedroom and the glazed door. It was he who replenished the coffeepot with boiling water from the kettle; and he who, when Madame Baron was busy in the bedrooms, prodded the potatoes with a fork to see if they were cooked enough.

"It's no trouble, I assure you. It gives me something to do."

He rarely spoke to Moise, and never said a word to Domb, who, the moment he had finished eating, went up to his room.

"Really," Madame Baron sighed, "he might have asked me for a tin box and had bread and butter for his supper like the others. Don't you agree, Monsieur Moise? As it is, I have to cook a hot dinner every evening, just for him!"

"Why not tell him that you won't go on doing it?"

"Somehow I don't like to. Silly of me, I know, but there it is! And, of course, it would be awkward because of my husband. He'd start asking questions. . . ."

To crown everything, since the cold snap had set in Elie had taken to wearing a frogged smoking jacket of purple velvet from morning till night. He had explained in detail how he had had it made for him in Budapest by Admiral Horthy's tailor, and obviously fancied himself in it, striking the poses of a Beau Brummell.

The worst day of all was a Tuesday. Baron was on duty on a day train and didn't come home till seven in the evening. On the previous day Elie had sensed something in the wind, and when, on Tuesday morning, he saw Madame Baron come back from her marketing with a large bunch of flowers, his curiosity became acute. So he laid an ambush—in other words, he left his bedroom door open and stayed lurking in the background. Valesco would be bound to pass the door sooner or later.

"Hello, old man!" Elie shouted to him. "Step in for a moment, will you?"

"Sorry, I'm in a hurry."

"I only want a word with you. What's happening here today?"

Valesco would have preferred to hold his peace, but he still owed Elie 300 francs, and saw no prospect of repaying them in the near future.

"Oh, it's Monsieur Baron's birthday."

"So that's it. Look here! Will you do me a small favor? I don't feel like going out myself. Would you mind going to the best florist in town and buying a bouquet? A really fancy one.

A hundred francs should be enough. Wait! I must give a present too. Let's see. . . . I don't think he has a fountain pen. Will you please buy one? Choose one of the best makes, please. Here's 300 francs for everything."

That morning there were frost flowers on the panes and the Rumanian's face was blurred almost out of recognition when Elie, watching from his window, saw him crossing to the streetcar stop.

A subtle, well-pleased smile lingered on Elie's lips when, after donning his gorgeous smoking jacket, he entered the kitchen, where Madame Baron was engaged in trussing two chickens. There was a knock at the hall door. It was the baker's boy, delivering two fruit tarts.

"Do please go back to your room, Monsieur Elie. Really, you'll make me quite annoyed if you stay in the kitchen."

And for once he complied with her request.

At noon Baron was still away. The midday meal was rushed through; Madame Baron and Antoinette were both in their best clothes, ready to go out as soon as it ended.

Was it that Elie found they weren't taking enough notice of him, and he resented being eclipsed by the domestic anniversary? Anyhow, as the meal was ending, he thought fit to say, rather loudly, to Valesco, who was seated beside him:

"Do you know, I've just thought of something rather interesting? They were talking in the papers about the difference between French and Belgian law. Well, suppose someone who's being proceeded against in Belgium by the French police commits a crime in Brussels, or some other Belgian town . . . ?"

He paused; the only sound to fill the silence was the clatter of knives and forks on plates—and for some reason it had a sinister effect, like the sound of a distant tocsin.

"You don't understand? What I mean is, that a man who's liable to the death penalty in France might happen to commit a crime in Belgium. In that case, it seems to follow that he should first be tried in Belgium, if it's in that country he's arrested. And it also follows, doesn't it, that he would serve his sentence in this country?"

His face was pale. His lips had an odd twist—but, at a stretch, it might have passed for a smile. And he looked genuinely pleased when he saw that Antoinette was smiling.

Moise straightened his back and looked him in the face.

"Would you be good enough to change the subject?"

He didn't dare persist, and turned his eyes away, but there was still a flicker of some curious emotion in the pupils.

The table was cleared more quickly than usual. Domb was the first to leave; then Valesco went to his bedroom. Madame Baron was starting to go up the stairs when Moise, putting on his student's cap, walked past her on his way to the front door.

"Monsieur Moise!" she called.

"Yes? All right, I'm coming."

They talked in whispers on the landing, and Elie, left by himself in the kitchen, strained his ears in vain to catch what was being said. A minute later he knew. There was little that escaped him. No sooner had Madame Baron and her daughter left the house than Moise, instead of settling to work in his room, brought his manuals and notebooks to the kitchen.

Without a word he seated himself in the armchair, Elie's usual place when Baron was out, and started jotting down rows of figures.

Elie put some coal on the fire, poked it noisily, then drew up a chair beside it. Smiling, he said:

"You've been told to keep an eye on me. Are they afraid I may steal something?"

Moise pretended not to hear.

"I'm not so dense as I may seem; I know you want to see the last of me. But you won't have to wait much longer. Once the police have lost interest in me I'll be off—and you can have your harem to yourself!"

The Polish Jew slowly raised his head. There was no trace of anger in the pale, staring eyes—and this made what followed all the more impressive.

"If you don't keep your dirty mouth shut," he said, "I'll bash your face in!"

Though smaller than Elie, he had a tougher build, and looked quite capable of putting the threat into execution. After he had spoken, the pencil could be heard biting into the paper, and the table started vibrating again.

Some minutes passed, and soon, for all his imperturbability, Moise looked up, puzzled by the long silence. He saw Elie sitting perfectly still, his eyes fixed on the red glow of the fire; his underlip was sagging, quivering.

Moise resumed his work, and after a while, without a sound, almost, it seemed, without the least displacement of air, Elie rose and walked out of the kitchen. The fire in his bedroom had gone out, but nonetheless he stayed there, sitting in front of the window.

Toward four, when the lamplighter was making his rounds, he saw two dim figures moving by, which he recognized as Antoinette and her mother. He heard the key turn in the lock, then footsteps in the hall. The two women had almost reached the kitchen door when there was a slight rattle of the mail slot; the evening paper had just been delivered.

Elie ran out and took it, then followed the women into the kitchen, where he found Moise gathering up his books and papers. The table was strewn with parcels of various shapes and sizes.

"Go upstairs and change your things," said Madame Baron to her daughter.

Before even taking off her hat she went to the stove, added a shovelful of coal, and put the kettle on to boil. Her cheeks were blue with cold; little beads of ice glittered on her fur stole.

"Has no one been here, Monsieur Moise?"

"No one."

Without a glance at Elie, she went upstairs to change her clothes, and a moment later Moise went up, too. The wicker chair creaked as Elie settled into it. The pages of the newspaper rustled. There was nothing of interest on the first or second page. But on the third he found a short paragraph headed THE MURDER ON THE PARIS EXPRESS.

There were only a dozen lines or so—which seemed to indicate that press and public had lost interest in the case.

The police authorities are continuing their investigation of this daring crime. Four days ago a cabaret dancer, Sylvie B., now residing in Brussels, was questioned, and she was able to furnish some useful information. It is now known that the murderer is a Turkish subject, named Elias Nagear, and that this young woman was his mistress. So far, however, all efforts to trace him have been unavailing. The police theory is that Nagear crossed the frontier into Germany before the crime was discovered. The young woman, Sylvie B., has been allowed bail.

Quite calmly Elie tore off this portion of the page and laid it on the table. His eyes were sparkling. He lit a cigarette and took long, luxurious puffs at it. As he did so, he listened to the noises in the house with growing impatience. The moment Madame Baron appeared in the doorway, her hands behind her back as she knotted her apron strings, he jumped up and almost shouted at her:

"Well? What did I tell you?"

His voice was shrill with triumph. He thrust the piece he had torn from the paper into her hand.

"Read this." And he couldn't help chuckling. "So they're looking for me now in Germany! Isn't it priceless!"

She ran her eyes over the article and, without thinking, handed it back to him; after this, though there was no need to do so, she poked the fire vigorously.

"So it's only a matter of a few days, and then, as I told you, I'll ..."

"Oh, keep quiet!" she exclaimed irritably. That reference to her daughter as the man's "mistress" was rankling in her mind.

"But it's such good news!" he insisted. "Now that they're looking for me in another country ..."

"For heaven's sake shut your mouth! And go back to your room. I don't want you here."

"Oh, if you're going to take it that way ..."

Tears were streaming down her cheeks as she went about her cooking. But she wept silently, after the manner of women no longer young. "This young woman was his mistress!" What would the neighbors think? They were sure to guess that "Sylvie B." stood for Sylvie Baron. And what would her husband say when he found out?

Antoinette came in and stared at her mother in amazement.

"What's wrong, Ma?"

"Nothing. Give me the flour."

"Has he been talking to you again?"

"No. Don't ask questions, please. My nerves are all in pieces."

"Will he have dinner with us tonight?"

"I don't see how we can prevent him."

Antoinette began unpacking the parcels. There were two pairs of socks, a black silk tie dotted with small white flowers, a smaller oblong package containing a narrow cardboard box.

"He'll be awfully pleased with this fountain pen," Antoinette remarked. "I wouldn't mind having one like it for my birthday, too."

It had cost sixty francs, and was a rather shoddy imitation of a well-known American make. The gold nib was only fourteen carats.

"Hand me the butter."

Meanwhile, Elie was reading again the article about himself. After he had learned it by heart he folded up the slip of paper and thrust it into a pocket of his velvet smoking jacket.

Domb came back and tramped up to his room. Moise went out and jumped into a moving streetcar, but was back again half an hour later.

There were all sorts of noises in the kitchen, and the house was full of unusual smells. For once, everybody kept to his room. Elie, who had drawn his curtains, held them a few inches apart and kept peeping out every time he heard footsteps in the street.

He was the first to hear the tinkle of the bell of a delivery boy's tricycle as it stopped outside, and he ran to the door, some small change in his hand.

It was the bouquet. He retreated to his room without having been seen from the kitchen and, after stripping the silver foil off the stems, placed the flowers in his water pitcher to keep them fresh. Valesco returned only a few minutes before seven. Elie, who had been watching, opened his door at once and took the little oblong package Valesco handed him.

"It's a first-rate make—the best I could find. A hundred and sixty francs. If the nib doesn't suit, it can be changed."

In the kitchen Madame Baron kept wiping her eyes with her apron. She wasn't actually shedding tears, but try as she could to prevent it, her eyes kept filling.

"He'll be here any moment now," she said.

She picked up the flowers that were lying in the sink, shook off the water, and arranged them in two vases. This evening the table was laid with a red-and-white-checked tablecloth, which enhanced the festive look of the room. Antoinette had disposed the presents in a little pile beside Baron's plate.

"Hadn't you better powder your face, Ma?"

"Does it show—that I've been crying?" Then she added rather sadly: "Hasn't Sylvie sent him anything at all, not even a birthday card?"

Elie watched the streetcar come to a stop. The windows were misted over and the body of the vehicle hid the people getting down from it. When it started again, with the usual clanging of its bell, he saw Baron crossing the street.

The rattle of a key. Heavy footsteps in the hall. Holding his door ajar, Elie heard Antoinette say:

"Happy returns, Pa."

There followed a sound of kisses, a confused murmur of voices. Upstairs, too, on the dark landing, the young men were leaning over the banisters, listening to the noises on the ground floor.

Elie was the first to enter the kitchen, his huge bouquet in one hand, the tiny package in the other.

"Monsieur Baron, please accept my wishes for many happy returns of the day."

The bouquet was far too grandiose for the humble little kitchen, and, grasping it awkwardly between his stubby fingers, Baron gazed at it with stupefaction. At last he stammered out some words:

"Really, Monsieur Elie, I don't know what came over you! It's much too fine for the likes of me."

He turned the small package over in his hands, at a loss what to say or do. Then, lumbering up to Elie, he kissed him, once on each cheek—or, rather, brushed it with his bristly mustache.

"Well, I must say, I never expected . . ."

Madame Baron went into the hall.

"Monsieur Moise! Monsieur Domb! Monsieur Valesco! Dinner's waiting."

The socks were unpacked, and duly approved; and then the necktie. But when Baron undid Elie's package he went into transports of delight.

"Why, it's a 'Parker'! A real one, not an imitation!"

While Elie beamed, Antoinette, looking thoroughly unhappy, reached toward the other fountain pen, which was still in its wrappings. But her father noticed the gesture.

"What are you up to, you little rogue?"

He was in high good humor. But when he opened the box and saw the other pen, the sixty-franc one, his face fell for a moment, and he didn't know what to say. Pulling himself together, he remarked cheerfully:

"Well, well, it never rains but it pours, as they say, and if I lose Monsieur Elie's . . ."

Madame Baron was busy with her saucepans.

Clicking his heels punctiliously, Domb bowed to the company, then handed Baron a horseshoe tiepin.

"I wish you a very happy birthday," he said gravely, "and many more to come. And may I take this opportunity of assuring you that I shall never forget the hospitality I have enjoyed under this roof?"

Valesco hurried in, and presented Baron with a briar pipe.

For some reason Baron did not give them the accolade he had bestowed on Elie—perhaps because neither young man came near enough.

Moise was the last to enter, and as he shut the door behind him he said:

"Happy birthday, Monsieur Baron."

He gave no excuse for failing to bring a present; everyone knew he was too poor. When he was placing his tin box on the table, Madame Baron tapped him on the shoulder.

"Not tonight! . . . Bless my soul, what's come over the boy?"

Blushing, Moise sat down at his place and stowed the box under his chair. Baron surveyed the company with an all-embracing smile.

"I am deeply touched . . ." he began.

Everyone fell silent—with the exception of Elie, who remarked:

"In my country, the birthday of the master of the house is the great event of the year. Even the servants bring presents. . . ."

For once, soup had been omitted from the menu, as being

too ordinary, not to say vulgar. Madame Baron placed the chickens on the table, and her husband rose to his feet to carve them.

"No! Let me."

Elie again! Antoinette's face was pale and set. Under the table she was giving little kicks to Moise, who was staring glumly at his plate. Madame Baron was too busy at the stove to be able to sit down.

"You, Moise, should know the rites and ceremonies," Elie observed as he plied the carving knife. "The Jews have all sorts of quaint, elaborate customs. . . . Say, Madame Baron, haven't you any candles?"

She looked around quickly.

"What do you want candles for?"

"We'd need . . . How old are you today, Monsieur Baron?"

"Fifty-two."

"Fifty-two candles. I don't suppose you could run to that. But in my country we always have the full number. At a certain moment of the evening all the lights are switched off, and . . ."

Moise gave him a hard stare. Elie hesitated, smiled, stopped talking. But five minutes later he was rattling away again.

"If there'd been any way of getting the ingredients, I'd have made you a Turkish pudding. My sister's a real good hand at it, but I'm not too bad myself."

"What's it like?" asked Baron.

"Well, for one thing, we flavor it with flowers. They have a much more delicate taste than jam."

"What? Do you mean to say you eat flowers?"

"No, it's an extract of flowers we use."

"What's wrong, Antoinette? Off your feed?"

To please her father she took a mouthful of chicken. Domb was staring glumly at the wall in front of him; Moise's brows were deeply furrowed. Only Valesco made some attempt at cheerfulness.

"I hope you'll come to Istanbul one day, Monsieur Baron. We should be delighted to put you up, and I'd show you the sights."

"Me go to Turkey? What an idea!"

"Why not? It only takes a day, by air."

While she stirred a sauce, Madame Baron, too, was casting angry glances at him, trying to make him shut up. But he appeared not to understand.

"The Turks are the most hospitable people on earth. Once you've stepped into a Turkish house you're its lord and master, and there's nothing they won't do for you."

"Even if you ain't asked in?" Baron naïvely inquired.

He hadn't meant it humorously, and was quite startled when Antoinette went into peals of laughter, so violent that she seemed on the point of choking. She rose abruptly and, turning her back on the others, spat out what she had in her mouth into her napkin. She was still laughing when she returned to her place, her lips twisting in queer grimaces, tears welling in her eyes.

Elie went on quite calmly.

"Yes, it sounds unlikely, doesn't it? But I can give you actual instances. Before the Great War my father had once been the guest of a Russian nobleman. After the Revolution the Russian came to Constantinople, as Istanbul was then called. Well, he stayed five years under our roof."

Antoinette was becoming hysterical; it was impossible to say if she was laughing or crying, and her father turned on her severely.

"Really now! How dare you behave like that when Monsieur Elie's talking? . . . Please continue, Monsieur Elie."

"That's the kind of thing you Westerners can never understand. My mother and sister have hardly any money left, but if someone came to see them and mentioned he was a friend of mine, they . . ."

"Antoinette!" said Baron sharply. "If it wasn't my birthday, I'd send you off to bed."

His wife snorted angrily. "I'd like to see you try it!"

Never had his wife talked to him in that tone before—anyhow in public. He blushed to the tips of his ears and started shoveling food into his mouth, hardly conscious of what he was doing. . . .

As usual, Domb was the first to get up and go.

"Them Poles are a stuck-up lot," Baron remarked as the door closed behind him. "Not a bit like the Turks. They seem to think they're doing you a favor every time they wish you 'Good morning.' Another thing I don't like in them is their way of treating Jews, even the Jews of their own country. When all's said and done, isn't Monsieur Moise just as much a Pole as he?"

He gazed at Moise, who, however, kept his mouth firmly shut.

"Where's your ma got to?" he asked Antoinette.

She went out and found Madame Baron sobbing to herself at the foot of the stairs.

"Don't bother about me," she snuffled. "I'll be all right soon. Tell them I'm coming back in a minute."

Antoinette could contain herself no longer.

"Listen, Ma! He's got to go. If he doesn't leave the house, I won't stay here a day longer. . . . Did you read that piece about him in the paper?"

"So he showed it to you, too?"

"Yes. He called me down on purpose. Wasn't it awful what they said about Sylvie's being his . . . his 'mistress'?"

When they returned to the kitchen, Moise was just leaving, and Valesco was waiting for a pretext to follow suit. Baron had taken a bottle of the Luxembourg liqueur from the cupboard, and Elie had moved to the empty place beside him.

"Here's luck! And here's the best to Turkey!"

"The best to Belgium!"

"Oh, dear! Pa's been drinking!" Antoinette whispered to her mother.

They cleared the table while the two men continued their drinking. Elie was very flushed, and Baron in a state of noisy animation that his wife knew only too well.

"How did you know I specially wanted a 'Parker'?"

"Oh, a little bird told me. . . ."

They roared with laughter. There was a constant clatter of plates and dishes in the background, and presently Madame Baron poked the fire for the last time, saying to Antoinette:

"Go to bed now. We'll finish washing up tomorrow."

Planting herself in front of the stove, her arms akimbo, she eyed the two men disapprovingly.

"Another glass, Monsieur Elie? Yes, yes, I insist. It isn't my birthday every day."

"What a good friend you are to me, Monsieur Baron! Do you know, I took a liking to you the very first day we met. To your wife, too. But that's not the same thing. It's never quite the same thing with women, is it—or isn't it? There's no friend like a man friend, eh?"

Vaguely conscious of Madame Baron's gaze intent on him, he made an effort to sober up, but without avail.

"And when you vish't us in Turkey, old man . . ." he began thickly.

And Baron, who was almost beginning to believe it, cut in cheerfully:

"Yes, yes. I suppose, one of these days . . ."

10

Valesco had the habit of hanging his shaving mirror on the window fastener for his morning shave. On this particular morning the sight of the children lining up at the school gate, and of an old fellow, who daily caught the 8:05 streetcar, waiting at the stop, told him the exact hour. Otherwise the street was almost empty, and the few passers-by were preceded by little blobs of mist formed by their breath.

When, after finishing his left cheek, Valesco was starting on his right, he noticed three men get off the streetcar and scan the house numbers. One of them was fat, and his unbuttoned overcoat displayed a gold watch chain looped across his vest. He wore his hat well back on his head and was smoking a big briar pipe.

One could tell he was the man in charge, and when he had spotted Number 53 he indicated it to the others with an upward nudge of his chin and a long stare, in the course of which he saw Valesco at the second-floor window. But the lace curtain prevented him from seeing more than the dim outline of a man's body.

He said something to the smaller of his two companions, a middle-aged man with a drooping mustache, who seemed to feel the cold, because he kept both hands thrust deep into the pockets of his tightly buttoned overcoat. After that the small man started pacing up and down outside the grocery, while the other two crossed the street.

Valesco waited to hear the doorbell ring, since he was convinced that these two men were coming to Number 53. But there was no ring, and, bringing his face closer to the window, he saw them going around to the back of the row of houses, presumably to make sure there was no exit there.

When they returned, their shoes were white with frost—which showed they had been walking in the rank grass of the field behind the house.

Another confabulation followed. The little man looked so perished with cold that Valesco felt quite sorry for him. The fat man, after a moment's indecision, turned into the grocery, and remained there a good five minutes. After he came out, the grocer's wife could be seen peeping excitedly from her window in the direction of Number 53. Valesco decided it was time to take action.

He went out to the landing and shouted: "Madame Baron!"

"What do you want? Hot water?"

"No. I want you to come up and see something."

But, as ill luck would have it, when he went back to the window, followed by Madame Baron, the fat man was already shaking hands with the small one; after which, looking pleased with himself, he moved off in the direction of town. The third man walked slowly across the street.

"Why did you call me?"

"You saw those men, didn't you?"

"Yes—what about them?"

"They're police officers; I'd swear to it. They've interviewed the grocer, and that little fellow keeps watching the house all the time. And I'm pretty sure the third man has gone to the back, and is keeping watch there, too. The big fellow who's just gone must be a superintendent."

Madame Baron stayed for some minutes, peeping from under cover of the curtain. Two streetcars came to the stop, but the little man didn't budge.

Valesco pointed downward.

"Is he up?"

"No. He sat up with my husband, drinking, till three in the morning, and he's sleeping it off."

There were heavy footsteps on the stairs; Domb was going out. Madame Baron asked anxiously:

"Don't you think we ought to tell him?"

"What's the use? He loathes Elie, anyhow."

The street door opened, and footsteps rang on the frozen sidewalk. The little man whipped out a notebook, looked hard at something in it, then hurried along on the other side of the street, parallel with Domb, staring hard at him.

"What did I tell you?"

He went only a hundred yards or so; then, reassured, no doubt, retraced his steps to the iron pillar that marked the streetcar stop.

"Now, Madame Baron, if you'll kindly leave me for a moment, I'll finish dressing."

Madame Baron found Antoinette in the kitchen, having her breakfast, and her first idea was to say nothing. Nor did her daughter make any remark, but there was a questioning look in her eyes—which gave the impression of having grown much bigger during the last few days.

"I think today will see the end of it," said Madame Baron with a sigh as she took her shopping basket from the cupboard. "And I must say I won't be sorry. . . . Is Pa still asleep?"

Antoinette nodded.

"I'd like it to be all over before he comes downstairs. There's a policeman watching in front of the house, and another at the back."

The girl's face grew rigid and she seemed unable to swallow the piece of bread she had just put in her mouth.

"I wonder," her mother continued, "if we should warn him. When I went to see him just now he was sleeping like a log. You could tell he'd had a drop too much last night. He was lying face downward, and snoring hard."

After thinking for a moment, she tiptoed up the stairs and tapped at the door of Moise's room. He opened at once. His hair unbrushed, the collar of his overcoat turned up, he had already started his day's work.

"Don't make a noise." She pointed to the wall between his room and the one where her husband was sleeping. Then she opened the window in the roof, but the eaves made it impossible to see down into the street. "No, you'll have to come downstairs," she murmured.

Moise followed her obediently. On the second-floor landing she turned in to Valesco's room. He had finished dressing and was back at his observation post at the window.

"Is he still there?"

Instinctively, they spoke in hushed tones, like people in a house of mourning. Madame Baron pointed to the man in the black overcoat, who was stamping his feet to keep them warm, his eyes still fixed on the house.

"That's a policeman. There's another at the back."

Moise avoided uttering Elie's name.

"Does *he* know?" he whispered.

"No. He's asleep. He was so drunk last night that he went to bed with his shoes on."

Antoinette had joined them, and was watching the plain-clothesman from the other window. The deeper he thrust his hands into his overcoat pockets, the more his shoulders seemed to shrink together.

"We'd better not hang around the windows," Madame Baron said. "Come along, Antoinette."

Moise went out first.

"You'll keep your eye on him, Monsieur Valesco, won't

you?" Madame Baron said over her shoulder, and the young man nodded.

In the kitchen she poured a cup of coffee and handed it to Moise.

"Drink it while it's hot. . . . Now tell me, what would you do in my place?"

Surprisingly enough, no one seemed in the least excited. But there was something sinister about their calmness that recalled to Madame Baron that day of evil memory when a German advance guard entered Charleroi and some twenty neighbors had gathered in the Barons' cellar. Then, too, there had been the same feeling of helplessness, of being at the mercy of events, and now and again one of them would go to the narrow, grated window, flush with the sidewalk, and watch a troop of cavalry clattering down the street.

"Really, it's my husband I'm most concerned about. There's no knowing how he'll take it, if he finds out all of a sudden like. . . ."

"What times does he go on duty?" Antoinette asked.

"Not till three. I only hope he'll go on sleeping. . . . Monsieur Moise, don't you think someone ought to warn him? Monsieur Elie, I mean. I don't feel up to it myself. When I think that it's perhaps the last time in his life he'll have a proper bed to sleep in . . ."

"Are you quite sure that man in the street is a policeman?"

"Monsieur Valesco says he is."

Moise felt in his pockets, then blushed and asked:

"Can I have a franc, please?"

A moment later he went out, leaving the door "to"—as Madame Baron termed it; that is to say, without letting the latch go quite home. Valesco, from his vantage point, saw him hurry across the street and noticed that the man in the overcoat gave a start and fished out his notebook at once.

Moise entered the grocery. By straining his eyes, Valesco

could still just make him out behind the dingy panes. He stayed there several minutes, during which the man in the overcoat studied his notebook.

Valesco hurried down to hear the news when he saw Moise running back across the street.

"He's a policeman, all right. The big one, who's gone, asked if you'd had a new lodger for the last fortnight or so. The grocer's wife said she couldn't be sure, but it was quite likely, since she'd seen a light in the ground-floor room."

"Have a cup of coffee, Monsieur Valesco. Antoinette, go and get the bottle of rum. It'll do us all good, a drink of something strong."

It was a sunny morning, and there were patches of moisture on the white walls of the back yard. But the block of ice like a cannonball—from Moise's broken pitcher—was still practically intact.

"I'll go and see if he's waked up."

Madame Baron walked boldly into Elie's room, and stood beside the bed. He was sound asleep, the sheets and blankets tossed back in disorder. A stale smell of drink hovered in the air, mingling with fumes from the stove and the pungent odor of warm linoleum. Still in a drunken stupor, he was evidently quite unconscious of her presence.

"Well?" Antoinette asked when her mother came back to the kitchen.

"Oh, he's asleep. Somehow I couldn't bring myself . . . But really, he ought to be told. Monsieur Moise, won't you do it—just to please me?"

Moise remained silent. Valesco prudently slipped out of the kitchen; he had no wish to be saddled with this unpleasant job, so he returned to his post behind the curtain.

The street was still almost empty. Sometimes a streetcar went by, bathed in sunlight, but with its windows frosted over. The distant stridence of a tin trumpet could be heard down on the left; the vegetable man was making his rounds. The police officer had lighted a pipe, and smoke was mingling with the white cloud of his breath.

The air was calm and clear, and the least sound evoked an echo, as on the fringes of a mountain lake. A rumbling high in air announced the passage of a train of skips on the aerial tramway. A little locomotive, too, could be heard puffing and blowing on a mine siding, and emitting a high-pitched whistle every time it made a move.

The plainclothesman was waiting for someone or something, it seemed, because he now kept throwing glances in the direction of town. Madame Baron started to peel potatoes, while Antoinette, forgetting for once to tidy up the bedrooms, stood with her back to the stove, hugging her knitted shawl around her breast. Suddenly she asked:

"Are you quite sure there's someone in the field behind?"

"Well, Monsieur Valesco saw the other policeman going that way."

"Because, if there wasn't, *he* could climb over the wall. And once he'd crossed the railway line . . ."

The policeman had been at his post for over an hour, and Elie was still asleep. The sickly sweet odor of hot rum pervaded the kitchen. Even Antoinette had had some.

"Take a glass upstairs to Monsieur Valesco," her mother said. "There's no fire in his room, and it's perishing by that window." Then she plucked at Moise's sleeve. "For goodness' sake say something! What do you think I ought to do? I'm a bundle of nerves, really, but I have to hold myself in because of Antoinette." Her lips were quivering; she seemed on the brink of tears.

Suddenly she gave a start; her cheeks grew pale.

"Listen!"

A car had stopped outside. There was the sound of someone walking briskly up the steps, a rattle of the mail slot.

"*You* go and open. I don't feel up to it."

The door opened just enough to let someone enter and to

143

give a glimpse of a taxi drawn up outside, its windows flashing in the level light. There was a click of high heels on the tiles.

Sylvie burst into the kitchen, bringing with her a gust of icy air. Without even pausing to kiss her mother, she asked excitedly:

"Has *he* gone?"

Tactfully, Moise had remained outside, in the hall, but Madame Baron called him in, perhaps because she was afraid of being alone with her daughter. Sylvie unbuttoned her coat and poured herself some rum, without troubling to get a clean glass.

"So he's still here! Didn't Antoinette get my letter?"

"Don't talk so loud. Your pa's upstairs."

From this she gathered that her father had been kept in the dark. But that was a side issue, and she had no time to waste on it.

"Anyhow, *they* haven't been here yet, have they?"

"There's been a policeman in front of the house all morning, and another at the back."

"Did they come from Brussels?"

"How do I know? The man in front hasn't moved once. Monsieur Valesco's keeping an eye on him, from his window."

Sylvie ran up the stairs and entered the young man's room without knocking. He looked around and bowed to her hastily.

"Is that him? That little fellow?"

"Yes. He's just taken the mumber of your taxi."

Sylvie had told the taxi driver to wait, and he was now pacing up and down the sidewalk in front of the house.

Valesco asked: "Have you come from Brussels?"

She walked out of the room without answering. All her movements were brisk, decided. She passed her sister on the stairs without a word. Greatly impressed, Madame Baron watched her activities from the kitchen, and sighed.

"I wonder what she means to do."

Moise said confidently:

"Oh, she knows what she's about, and she'll handle it much better than we would."

But everyone gave a start—Valesco as well as the two in the kitchen—on hearing a familiar creak; Elie's door had just been opened. It closed again immediately, and nothing more could be heard.

Elie had moved in his sleep and was sheltering his eyes with his arm from the sunlight flooding in through the window.

"Get up at once!" Sylvie shook his arm vigorously.

He groaned, and shifted his position again. When at last he opened his eyes and saw the girl gazing down at him, he muttered:

"What on earth . . . ?"

His head was throbbing, and he could remember nothing of the night before. There was a foul taste in his mouth, and he felt that his neck had gone stiff again. He stared vacantly at Sylvie.

"You got my message, didn't you?" she said. "Well?"

There was a vicious edge to her voice; no compassion in her eyes. In a half-dream, Elie watched the sunlight playing on her hair, rippling along the sleeve of her fur coat.

"Get up, damn it! Don't you realize they're after you, and they'll be here any minute?"

He leaped out of bed and landed on his feet with the agility of a monkey.

"What's that?" Suspicion flickered in his eyes.

"Don't be a fool! I tell you, the game's up. They're at the door."

His face grew contorted with fury.

"Ah, so you betrayed me, did you?"

"Betrayed you, indeed! Stop playacting and get your clothes on."

He stared at her for a moment, then exclaimed:

"I've got it! It's just a trick of yours to get me out of this house. Very clever of you, but—nothing doing!"

145

Then he noticed the taxi drawn up outside, and he went to the window. Sylvie pointed.

"Do you see that fellow there, beside the streetcar stop? He's a plainclothesman."

Even now Elie seemed only half convinced. He went to the basin, gargled, and spat the water out. Never had his features looked so angular, his cheeks so pale and wasted.

"Yes," he said bitterly, "I understand it all now."

"Good! In that case, hurry up and get dressed."

"Yes," he said again, "and, what's more, I know why you gave me away. For money, of course. You'd do anything for money, wouldn't you?"

"Oh, stop that damn nonsense!"

"And I should have guessed that was your game when you tricked me into coming here."

She raised her arm to slap him, but he looked so frail and wretched in his draggled pajamas that she let it fall again.

"Get dressed!"

"Don't you order me around! I'll do what I damn well please—and I warn you, you'll regret it!" He watched Sylvie from the corner of an eye to see what effect his threat had had on her, but she had her back to him and was staring out the window.

The previous evening, she had been summoned to the headquarters of the Brussels Criminal Investigation Department and confronted by three police officers. Two of them were smoking pipes. The detective who had questioned her at the cabaret was sitting on a corner of the table, beside a Belgian police superintendent. The third man, who kept pacing up and down the room, was a member of the Paris CID.

"Take a seat, Mademoiselle. Now let's hear why you told us all those lies. . . ."

She had found time to glance at the papers strewn on the table and to notice a letter headed "Station Café, Charleroi."

With an effort she conjured up a smile, an air of injured innocence.

"And wouldn't you have done the same thing in my place?" she asked breezily.

The three men exchanged glances; then they, too, grinned, taken by her effrontery.

For three days Sylvie had been expecting this to happen. She knew the porter at the Palace had seen her taking away Elie's luggage; and not only the porter but the shoeshine boy, who had helped to load it into a taxi. And because it's always the same taxis that line up outside a big hotel, there had been no difficulty in tracing the one she'd taken. The trail led to Charleroi, first to the station café, then to Number 53, Rue du Laveu.

"Is he still lodging with your parents?"

"I haven't any idea. . . . And that's the gospel truth."

"Are you aware that we could arrest you for aiding and abetting?"

Her eyelids fluttered; she smiled again.

"I acted as anyone in my place would have acted—that's all I have to say. By the way, I can assure you that my parents haven't the faintest notion who he is."

That closed the proceedings. The three men exchanged glances once more, but could think of nothing else to ask. The only question was: Should she or should she not be taken into custody? The French police officer shrugged his shoulders to show it was a matter of indifference to him.

"All right, you can go now. But hold yourself in readiness to appear whenever we need you."

"Any objection to my going to Charleroi?"

The three men conferred.

"No. You may go there if you want to."

It was eleven at night when Sylvie left police headquarters. She felt certain they were at this moment telephoning the

Charleroi police, telling them to keep watch on the house—if, indeed, they weren't doing that already. She drove to the Merryland and had a whispered conversation with Jacqueline. After that she danced, stayed up well into the small hours drinking champagne with a shipowner from Antwerp, and day was breaking when she changed her dress.

Now Elie was eying her with hatred and disgust. He saw her in profile, sunlight playing on her hair, a fainter sheen on the tightly drawn silk stockings—stockings he had given her!

"Get dressed!" she repeated wearily.

Then she walked out of the room, closing the door behind her. In the kitchen her mother gave her a questioning look; then asked:

"Well? What did he say?"

Antoinette's eyes were fever-bright, her lips tight-set, and she gazed intently at her sister. But all that Sylvie, who was warming her hands at the fire, found to reply was:

"What did you expect him to say?"

Valesco entered and, without being asked, helped himself to rum. Again Madame Baron was reminded of those chaotic days of 1914, when all the conventions of ordinary life went by the board.

"The cop's still hanging around outside," the Rumanian informed them. "But his nose isn't quite so red, because he's in the sun now."

He glanced at the clock, which showed half past ten. Suddenly Madame Baron stopped peeling her potatoes and said to Antoinette:

"I'm so afraid your pa may wake up. Go and see if he's still asleep."

Obediently Antoinette went to the door and tiptoed up the stairs.

"Are you sure there isn't anything we can do . . . ?" Madame Baron began tentatively, but refrained from looking at her daughter.

"No," said Sylvie peremptorily. "It's no use looking for trouble."

"If it wasn't for that policeman at the back . . ." Valesco murmured. "But they're taking no chances."

Sometimes a faint sound from Elie's room made them cast nervous looks at each other.

"I know what I'd do in his place," Valesco added.

Madame Baron looked him in the eyes.

"Yes? And *what* would you do?"

Valesco made the gesture of a man pointing a revolver at his forehead. Madame Baron shuddered, and poured herself some rum. None of them was conscious of drinking—but the bottle was half empty already. Antoinette came back.

"Pa asked me what the time was. I told him it was only eight, and he went to sleep again."

Like her mother, she refrained from looking at Sylvie, who was the only one to seem quite unperturbed. Moise, however, kept stealing glances at her, after each of which he promptly turned away.

"Ssh! He's coming!"

A door creaked. Sunlight was pouring in through the narrow window over the front door, filling the hall with a luminous haze, through which Elie's spare form showed in dark relief. They saw him linger for a moment outside his door, then walk quietly toward the kitchen.

The only sound was a choking sob from Madame Baron.

They could hardly recognize the man who halted in the doorway, so changed he seemed. There was something terrifying in the preternatural calm that had descended on him. But the red-rimmed eyes were dark with scorn and hatred as they roved from one face to the other, and there was a bitter twist to his lips.

"Well? Are you satisfied—now?" he asked with a harsh laugh, and reached toward the bottle.

Never had the little kitchen seemed so cramped. They were

149

huddled up together, afraid to meet each other's eyes. The sun had reached the block of ice in the yard, and Antoinette, who was nearest the window, could see it sparkling with broken lights.

Sylvie turned on him.

"Keep your mouth shut!"

Beads of sweat glistened on Elie's upper lip, and he had cut his chin shaving. He had on the stylish gray suit that he had worn on board the *Théophile-Gautier*.

He looked out into the yard and, tilting his head back, measured the height of the white wall, above which stretched a dazzling expanse of bright-blue sky. Madame Baron started sobbing again, and moaned:

"*Do* speak, someone. . . . Isn't there anything we can do?"

She couldn't bring herself to look at Elie. Moise had turned away and was staring at the wall. Valesco made a quick move, and ran up to his room.

"There's nothing to be done," said Sylvie gravely. "If there had been, I'd have done it."

For some reason, Elie had drawn closer to Antoinette, and she did not move away. He fixed his eyes on her, and their expression was so strange that, when he made as if to lay his hand on her shoulder, the girl screamed and threw herself into her mother's arms.

Valesco came racing down the stairs.

"They're here!" he cried.

The engine of a car was throbbing outside the door. There was a clatter of footsteps on the sidewalk, a sound of voices. Elie swung around so quickly that everyone fell back in alarm, and just as the doorbell rang he dashed out and scrambled up the stairs.

"Oh, dear!" wailed Madame Baron, clasping Antoinette to her breast. "He'll wake your pa!"

Valesco remained in the kitchen, and it was Sylvie who

opened the door. Three dark forms could be seen outlined against the sunlight.

"So you got here first!" said one of the men, laughing. "Not been up to any tricks, I hope?"

The detective who had interviewed her at the Merryland promptly opened the first door, saw the suitcases marked "E.N.," and, stooping, looked under the bed.

"Where is he?"

The French police officer was smoking a cigarette on the doorstep, and appeared to take no interest in the proceedings.

"Upstairs," Sylvie replied.

They could see Madame Baron and Antoinette watching from the dimly lighted kitchen, and from their end the two women saw the superintendent take a revolver from his pocket and load it.

"You go in front." It was to Sylvie that the superintendent spoke, and without the least hesitation she started up the stairs.

On the landing she stopped and opened the doors of the bedrooms occupied by Domb and Valesco. Both were empty.

The little plainclothesman in the street had approached the house, and he, too, was clutching a revolver, concealed in his overcoat pocket.

"Don't be alarmed," Valesco murmured, looking at Madame Baron.

She tried to smile, and went on stroking Antoinette's red hair. In an agony of suspense, the girl was listening to the sounds upstairs.

"Ssh! Don't speak!" she whispered.

By now Sylvie and the two men had reached the top floor. Suddenly there was a scream, followed by a series of crashes, as if furniture were being thrown about, windows smashed.

A moment later came a sound of almost tranquil footsteps on the stairs. It was Sylvie coming back. She was very pale, and on entering the kitchen she walked straight to the window and pressed her forehead to the pane, which grew misted with her breath.

"What are they doing?"

The thuds were continuing, and now there were shouts as well.

"The last thing I saw of him"—Sylvie got the words out with an effort—"he was sitting on the edge of the roof. He seemed to go quite crazy all of a sudden, and they had a dreadful fight, rolling about on the floor. He broke loose and climbed out the window. They're trying to haul him back." She turned on the faucet, soaked her handkerchief in the ice-cold water, and dabbed her face.

Suddenly Madame Baron screamed:

"Antoinette!"

Moise sprang forward just in time to catch the girl, who had fainted.

"Lay her on the table."

In his haste Valesco upset the bottle of rum and knocked a glass to the floor. No one had any idea what to do next, until Madame Baron said:

"Vinegar . . ."

But just then there was a noise on the stairs, and she looked away from her daughter toward the hall. She had a glimpse of Elie's back, and didn't realize it was handcuffs that made him walk so awkwardly.

"She's coming to," said Moise, who was bending over Antoinette.

But Madame Baron had rushed out, followed by Sylvie, who was vainly trying to drag her back.

The three men stopped in the hall. Madame Baron, who was standing a couple of yards from Elie, seemed incapable of making the least movement, or getting a word out.

Elie's face was badly injured, his hair plastered on his forehead, his nose bleeding profusely—but what impressed her most was the change that had come to his eyes. They kept moving restlessly from one object to another, and had a curious blank intensity that reminded her of the eyes of certain caged animals she had seen in the zoo. In fact, it seemed that he failed to recognize her, or any of the others.

"Do wait a moment," she begged the police officers. "He can't go out in that state," and she edged past them into the bedroom.

Her husband was standing halfway down the stairs, but she paid no attention to his look of horrified inquiry.

The superintendent had got out his handkerchief and was stanching the flow of blood from a gash across his hand.

"Get his suitcases," he said to the plainclothesman, who had just come in.

Madame Baron returnd with a damp towel and started wiping Elie's face. It had all taken no more than a few minutes, but already quite a crowd had collected outside. A small boy, perched on the railing, was peeping in Elie's bedroom window.

Elie took Madame Baron's ministrations quite calmly, but blood kept oozing from the wounds as fast as she wiped it off.

At last the superintendent intervened, and gently thrust her aside. "Let him be, Madame. He's not badly hurt." To the men with him he added: "Get those people away. We don't want a crowd outside."

A moment later they heard a gruff voice in the street:

"Move on there! What are you hanging around for? There's nothing to see."

Now and then Baron took a cautious step down the stairs, moving like a man in a dream. What was happening passed his comprehension. He had only a shirt and trousers on, and slippers on his feet.

"Move on! Didn't you hear what I said?"

Of his own accord Elie started walking toward the door. He

had to stand back to let the man carrying his suitcases go out first. Sylvie's taxi and the police car were drawn up one behind the other.

"Shove him in!"

There was a shrill scream from the kitchen. Valesco, who was halfway down the hall, went no farther. Madame Baron stood beside him, the bloodstained towel in her hand, gazing toward the street.

After that events moved fast. The police officers and their prisoner crossed the zone of sunlight and vanished into the car. The Frenchman took the seat beside the driver. The door slammed, and some of the people outside ran after the car as it moved off, for a last glimpse.

Sylvie, to whom nobody was paying much attention, gave her mother a perfunctory kiss and stepped into the taxi.

All was over, but people were still hanging around the house, and Madame Baron shut the door. She seemed utterly worn out, hardly able to drag herself along. Her husband, as puzzled as ever, glanced into the empty bedroom, and his eyes fell on the pink-stained water in the basin.

At last he got some words out:

"What on earth happened?"

Children were scrambling onto the windowsill; it was Moise who had the presence of mind to think of closing the shutters. Valesco was trying to forget about the money he still owed Elie.

On the previous night, Elie's bouquet had been put in a pail and left in the pantry, to keep the flowers fresh. The water had frozen in the night, and they had to be thrown away.

11

The string of vehicles approaching La Rochelle was headed by a large open car, in which photographers rode. Following it in single file came fifty-three vehicles, all police vans, which had set out at dawn from the big prison at Fontevrault.

It was a fine, warm autumn morning, and the villages were bathed in sunlight. People came to their doorsteps to watch the gray, windowless vans, with armed guards posted beside the drivers, streaming past.

As the long procession slowed down on its way through La Rochelle, the photographers stood up in their car and took shots of it. Then came La Pallice, and the vans stopped on the North Quay, to the right of the harbor, across which fishing boats were gliding.

The crowd was kept back by a police cordon, which only those with special permits were allowed through. So there were few except reporters and photographers actually on the quay, where a tug was made fast in readiness to convey the prisoners to Ile de Ré, the first stage of their journey to the convict settlement.

"Where are the stars?" one of the photographers asked a policeman posted at the gangway.

"The what? Oh, yes, of course . . . Delpierre's in the second van I think."

Delpierre was a locksmith who had killed his wife and his five children with an ax.

"And Nagear?"

"Fourth or fifth van. You've seen his sister, haven't you? That's her, over there." He pointed to a tall girl in gray, who was standing in the front row of onlookers. The photographer ran across the open space toward her, but before he could aim his camera she had hidden her face with her gloved hand.

Her neighbors in the crowd began to eye her with interest, and noticed that she was carrying field glasses. The word was passed around that she was a relative of one of the prisoners.

The door of the first van opened. From each cell a man in ordinary clothes stepped out, hampered by shackles and hand-cuffs that constrained the movement of his arms. With a knapsack on his shoulder, a loaf of black bread under his arm, he slowly walked between the rows of reporters and was led by a guard to the back of the boat. There he squatted on the deck, blinking from the glare off the water.

Most of the convicts were in rags and advanced timidly, as if afraid of making some blunder and being reprimanded, perhaps struck. Some, however, faced the reporters with defiant eyes, a scornful curl of the lips.

"Look! That's him!"

Elie had on his gray suit, a black felt hat, and a well-cut raincoat. He took no notice of the bystanders and concentrated his attention on the shackles, which made his movements curiously ungainly. To make things worse, the big round loaf kept slipping from under his arm.

Only when he was on board, seated on the deck between two fellow convicts, did he look up and face the cameras pointed at him. Five hundred yards away a tall girl was fever-ishly trying to adjust the focus of her field glasses.

"He's smiling!" a reporter remarked.

Was it really a smile? That furtive ripple of his lips might have meant almost anything. Then he turned to the gray-haired prisoner on his right and began a conversation with him.

"Is that girl in gray really his sister?"

"Yes, and I've heard she's come all the way from Constantinople."

None of those present could remember the departure of a shipload of convicts having taken place in such perfect weather. Though autumn was well advanced, it was like a summer's day, the sky serenely blue.

And, a week later, when the final embarkation was about to take place, the fine spell still persisted. Drenched in sunlight, the white-walled house on Ile de Ré reminded one of well-washed sheets spread out to dry on a green meadow.

The curtain was rising on the second act. The convict ship, *La Martinière*, was anchored in the offing, surrounded by a swarm of fishing boats. All the rooms in all the hotels of the island were taken. In every café you could see newspapermen greeting each other; cameras lay on the billiard tables.

"Many relatives turn up this time?"

"Yes, and there's a whole tribe of gypsies."

The gypsies had tramped all the way from the Mediterranean coast to see off the patriarch of their clan. They had camped at the foot of the ramparts, and all day long wild-looking women and children were to be seen prowling about town, never addressing a word to anyone.

"Nagear's sister has come, too."

She had taken a room at the best hotel, and she, too, was to be seen walking on the sea front at all hours. She was still in her gray tailor-made outfit, and always wore gloves. She never talked to the other guests at the hotel and had her meals by herself, but on several occasions she had been noticed talking with members of the prison staff.

"Most likely she's trying to get some money through to him," someone observed.

That was so, and, though constantly rebuffed, she kept on trying. She even appealed for help to one of the reporters.

"You'll be in the front row, won't you, when they're marched on board? Do please slip this into his hand as he goes by."

She couldn't understand why everyone always refused, and her look conveyed what she thought of them. One morning she even buttonholed the governor of the Saint-Martin prison in the main street of the town. He took off his hat politely when she came up to him, but no sooner had she started to explain than, putting on his hat again, he walked away.

Even so she did not lose heart. She harried people with questions, as if they had nothing else to do but give her information.

"Tell me, please! Which road do they go down? Where is the public allowed to stand?"

She was told that windows overlooking the route taken by the prisoners could be rented, and she paid for one. But on learning that the Venetian blinds had to be kept closed when the men were passing, she returned to the house and insisted on having her money back.

Two smartly dressed men who had been hovering in the background promptly came forward and rented the window she had given up. One of them, she learned, was a brothel owner from Marseilles; the other, the brother of a man under sentence of transportation.

Everyone knew everybody else by sight, since they passed each other ten or a dozen times a day on the sea front. On the last morning, however, there was a newcomer—a woman in black who landed from the La Rochelle ferry, and looked around her with a bewildered air.

"Is this where the convicts go on board?" she asked the first person she met. "They haven't embarked yet, have they?"

By way of luggage she had only a handbag, and she carried it around with her all morning. When the clock struck twelve, she seated herself on the sea wall, opened the bag, and took out some food.

Elie's sister walked past her once or twice, and gave her a long look each time.

Meanwhile, the prisoners were being lined up in the prison courtyard for the final roll call. The prison buildings were built of the velvety-gray stone so much used in that part of France, and the sky above them was a dome of pale, translucent blue.

In an adjoining yard another parade was going on: of military police and guards, who were being given their final instructions for the voyage.

At the same time, squads of police were barring the approaches to certain streets, refusing access to all who were not provided with police passes. Esther found herself held up by one of them.

"But I tell you, you *must* let me through," she almost shouted at the policeman in charge. Then, calming down and pointing to a street bordered by tamarisk trees, she asked: "Will they come by that street?"

"Yes, Mademoiselle."

She had noticed a garden surrounded by a low wall halfway up the street, and saw that, by turning up a side street, she could approach it from behind.

On the stroke of one, the great gate of the prison swung open, and the first to emerge were some prison officials in dark clothes. They were followed by a long procession, like a funeral cortege, moving slowly between two lines of policemen holding back the crowd.

The district superintendent remarked to the prefect of the department, who was walking at his side:

"I'm pretty sure those gypsies will put in an appearance. The whole tribe put together to pay their fares here, so I'm told."

Escorted by Senegalese infantrymen, the 700 convicts advanced at a slow, funereal pace. All were wearing clogs, many of them for the first time. Each man had a knapsack on his back, a roll of bedding on his shoulder. Their civilian clothes had been taken from them and replaced by the convict garb of coarse brown serge, and they wore oddly shaped black caps.

As they were approaching the low wall, Esther's head bobbed up, her field glasses trained on the front ranks.

"Sergeant! Get that woman to clear off!" said the superintendent as he walked by.

The sergeant had only to give a glance, and the head ducked down again behind the wall. The superintendent explained to the man beside him:

"That's the sister of that young fellow Nagear. She wanted to slip some money to him."

"Nagear? Who's he?"

"He's the fellow who killed that Dutchman with a wrench on the Brussels express."

"Ah, yes, I remember."

Cameras clicked. The crowd surged forward and was hustled back again. Just then, on catching sight of the man for whom they were watching, the gypsies set up a long, shrill keening, a cry of desolation so intense that for a moment all seemed held in abeyance, all movement arrested.

But then the steady tramp started again, and soon they had reached the quay and the three tenders that were to take the prisoners out to *La Martinière*. Although as they passed up the gangways in single file they all looked much alike, one of the press photographers managed to recognize Elie, who was plodding ahead with the same slow, mechanical steps, the same look of sullen resignation on his face, as his companions.

A woman in black was dodging to and fro behind the

serried ranks of spectators, vainly trying to see over their shoulders, now and then plucking someone by the sleeve.

"Please, would you tell me, are they passing now? Yes? I do wish you'd let me squeeze in—or couldn't I have your place just for a moment?"

She ran a little farther along the quayside, only to come up once more against a solid wall of bodies.

"Couldn't you let me have a peep? Just a little peep? . . . Anyhow, you might tell me what they're doing. Are they going on board now?"

A group of young men brushed past her, with cameras under their arms. They had chartered a motorboat so as to be able to accompany the tenders out to *La Martinière*. The motorboat was alongside the quay, the engine turning over.

"Wait!" she called to them.

They stopped and stared at her, wondering who she was and what she wanted.

"I'm coming with you," she panted.

"Sorry, but we can't take passengers."

But already she had dumped her handbag on the edge of the quay and, stretching out her arms, was about to spring to the boat. There was a five-foot drop between her and the deck.

"Get back! You can't come with us."

The boat was beginning to draw away. She sprang clumsily forward and fell into the arms of a young reporter, who looked terribly embarrassed.

"Hurry up!" someone said. "There's no time to lose."

"Oh, I've left my bag!" she gasped.

But there wasn't time to turn back for it. The tenders were casting off, and the photographers wanted to be in front of them.

Upset by the motion of the boat, the woman sat down.

"Do you know who any of them are?" she asked the man beside her, who was putting film in his camera.

"Two or three."

"I wonder if you happened to see a young fellow among them—brown hair he has, and looks like a boy of sixteen, though he's really much older?"

"What's his name?"

But to that she gave no answer. They were moving past the tenders, and hundreds of convicts were looking down at the motorboat speeding seaward.

"Have their clothes been taken away?"

"Yes. They have only numbers now to distinguish them."

The skipper of the motorboat whispered in the ear of one of the reporters:

"Better keep an eye on her. I imagine she's a relative. Take care that she doesn't do anything silly—throw herself overboard, or something like that. There have been cases of that kind, you know."

Word was passed around, and they took turns sitting beside the elderly woman, who, however, showed no particular sign of emotion. One of them asked her:

"Is it one of the convicts you're interested in?"

She made a movement of her head, which might have been a nod.

"Perhaps we could help you. Is there anything you particularly want to know?"

"Do they have a very hard time out there? Can one send them comforts?"

The tenders had outpaced the motorboat, which was now bobbing in their wake. Sunlight played on the streaming lines of foam. Some fishing boats, too, were going out to sea; on the deck of one of them, the crew could be seen having a meal and passing a bottle of red wine from mouth to mouth.

"Can't we get a little closer?" the woman asked.

"Nothing doing, I'm afraid. Those tenders have the speed on us. But you'll have a good view of the prisoners when they're going up the Jacob's ladder."

"Well I never! Do they have to climb up a ladder?"

Her eyes were dry, and indeed she showed no signs of distress; and it was this strange calmness that alarmed the others. The skipper whispered to the man beside him:

"I once saw a woman jump overboard just when the convict ship weighed anchor."

As an extra precaution he detailed one of the crew to keep watch on their uninvited passenger.

"Why ever do they make them wear those horrid clothes?" she murmured. "A real shame I call it!"

One of the photographers, noticing her accent, remarked:

"You're Belgian, aren't you? I didn't know there were any Belgians in this bunch."

But she still refused to let herself be drawn out. She was wearing cotton gloves, shoes that were rather down at the heel, and obviously homemade stockings.

"How'll you manage about your bag?"

"My bag? I haven't thought about it. Anyhow, I'll be starting back this evening."

Evidently she was not concerned about the fate of her handbag. All the time her eyes were fixed on the tenders and the rows of heads showing above the rails, all in the same grotesquely shaped cloth caps.

"If only I had field glasses!" she sighed.

One of the crew handed her a pair, but she didn't know how to focus them, and after some vain attempts she gave them back.

The convict ship was looming up just ahead. A yacht glided past, with young men and women in white dresses lounging on the deck.

Someone said:

"Look! They're going on board now."

One of the tenders had made fast alongside the steamer and men could be seen climbing up the ladder. But when the motorboat approached, a peremptory blast from the ship's siren warned them to stand off. The sailor on duty beside the woman held himself in readiness to pounce on her if she made the least move.

Crowded together on the deck of a small fishing boat, the gypsies passed them. All were standing, craning their necks toward the convict ship, shading their eyes with their hands.

The photographers got busy.

"One more shot. Get as near as you can, skipper."

The sailor asked:

"Have you spotted him?"

But she kept silent. She had seen nothing except a number of men who, in the distance, all looked exactly the same, like a procession of black ants crawling up the ship's side. In her coat of dazzling white paint, bathed in sunlight, *La Martinière* might have been a luxurious yacht, and the sea was dappled with silvery glints.

"Let's go straight back to La Rochelle," a photographer said. "I mustn't miss my train."

For a good hour yet the convicts would go on streaming up the ladder, but it made a monotonous picture; a few dozen feet of film sufficed.

No more notice was taken of the woman in black, who remained seated on a hatch, a vague smile on her lips as she gazed across the sea. Only when they were making fast at La Rochelle and she went up to the skipper, opening a shabby black purse, did they notice her again.

"How much do I owe you?" she asked.

"Nothing at all. These gentlemen are paying for the trip."

She murmured some words of thanks; then inquired:

"How does one get to the station?"

"Walk along the wharf a hundred yards, and you'll find it right in front of you."

"Thank you . . . You're most kind. . . ."

And Madame Baron went on smiling to herself, perhaps because it was such an exceptionally fine day. They had told her that calm weather would prevail in the Atlantic. "Anyhow, that blanket looked nice and warm," she reflected.

The train did not leave till nine in the evening, and it was now only six. She had plenty of time to look around the town, or to stroll about the station. But she did neither. She settled down in the third-class waiting room, feeling a little ill at ease, perhaps because she didn't have her handbag with her. It had remained on the Ile de Ré. She bought a sandwich at the buffet, after first asking the price.

She did not notice Esther, who came back by the eight o'clock ferry and dined in the Refreshment Room.

The two women traveled in the same train, one in a second-class car, the other in a third. When the conductor came around to check her ticket soon after the train had left, Madame Baron happened to mention that her husband also was a conductor, for the Belgian railway; and when the train stopped at Niort, he moved her into an empty first.